SINGLE STROKE . . .

Crouched in the bushes, Tanaka Tom waited while the posse wended its way among the rocks and trees, climbing toward him. One by one they passed him by until a single rider remained. He drew even with Tom when the Samurai rose, the keen edge of his sword whistling through the air. Steel bit into flesh below the rider's ribcage, slicing the man in half. A shriek of agony issued from the toppled upper portion while his horse, bathed in blood, bolted. It lunged forward, trailing warm, moist coils of intestine, the lower half of the rider still firmly in the saddle.

Tanaka Tom, six-gun in his left hand, sword held high in his right, charged upward to the next man in line. As the gunslinger brought his gun into play, Tom's Colt roared and the big 255-grain slug smashed into the other man's chest, pulped bone and lung and drove life from him.

As the others opened fire, the Six-Gun Samurai automatically adjusted his own line of attack and moved in on a third victim.

"It's an ambush! My God, there must be a dozen of 'em!" one man cried in confused fright.

"Pull back," the leader ordered in a bull-throated roar. "Let's get outta here."

In seconds the disorganized posse had crashed through the trees to the road and headed back toward the junction, spurs digging painfully into horse flesh, as Tanaka Tom sent a pair of out-of-range revolver rounds after them to speed them on their way. . . .

The Six-Gun Samurai Series:

#4
SIX-GUN SAMURAI
KAMIKAZE JUSTICE.
Patrick Lee

PINNACLE BOOKS   NEW YORK

SIX-GUN SAMURAI #4: KAMIKAZI JUSTICE

Copyright © 1981 by Mark Roberts

An original Pinnacle Books edition, published for the first time anywhere.

First printing, August 1981

ISBN: 0-523-41416-1

Cover illustration by Bruce Minney

Printed in the United States of America

PINNACLE BOOKS, INC.
1430 Broadway
New York, New York 10018

This book is dedicated with gratitude to Howard and Chad Poyer of Seattle, whose time machine gave the author a pleasant journey back twenty years for a magnificent Sunday afternoon—the hot sand and brilliant colors of *La Fiesta Brava.* Thanks again.

Prologue

Standing on the Charleston, South Carolina, dock, looking upward at the frigate's towering masts and spars, the young boy's eyes widened with wonder. Could it all really be true? Thomas James Fletcher, Midshipman, United States Navy? That was a lot of handle to tag onto so small a boy. In two days he would reach his twelfth birthday and the day following he would sail on this mighty ship to New York, where he would sign his warrant as midshipman and take the oath.

His appointment to the navy had come through the efforts of a neighbor, Issac Tomlinson, son of an influential man in state and national affairs. The Tomlinson plantation adjoined the smaller holdings of the Fletcher family along the Savannah River, near Wentworth, Georgia. Young Issac had watched Tom Fletcher grow up. When the lad expressed a desire to go to sea, Issac, a graduate of the U.S. Military Academy, and his father, Squire Tomlinson, used their influence to insure that the experience would be one that promised a future as well as adventure.

The about-to-be midshipman—known as T. J. to his father, Thomas James to his mother, and Tommy to his friends—had talked of nothing else, during the last six months since acknowledgment of the appointment had come from Washington City. The year was 1853 and, although he didn't know it at the time, Tommy Fletcher would soon set sail on an historic voyage with Commodore Perry to the islands of Japan.

Young Tommy Fletcher lived in a world of high adventure on the vast seas of the world, but nothing like that which befell him in the land of *Nippon*. Assigned to the American Mission established at *Edo*, the seat of government—as opposed to the capital at Kobi where the Emperor was in residence—the boy soon found he liked the Japanese and quickly adapted parts of their lifestyle. The Mission's purpose was to coordinate activities for the coaling and trade stations opened in the ports of Shimota and Hakodate. Not everyone in the ruling class accepted the decision of the shogun and Emperor to end the Act of Exclusion and admit Western barbarians to the realm of the Sublime Morning Sun. Among them, one powerful Daimyo employed the services of the cultlike order of assassins, the *Ninja*, to remove these offensive pale-skinned barbarians. In the raid on the American Mission, only Tommy Fletcher escaped alive.

Cold, nearly naked—clad only in a pair of the half-trousers affected by the lower classes of Japan—Tommy found himself alone and helpless in a hostile city. Now his interest in things Japanese came to his aid. He had a quick ear for languages and a retentive mind. As he learned to speak the native tongue, he was able to compete with other dockyard waifs for odd jobs among the ship builders and fishermen. Considered a "Hairy Ainu" from the northern islands, he met with grudging acceptance. Then one night, following a scuffle with a band of beggar boys, Tommy ran, literally, head-on into Tanaka Nobunara, a young samurai.

The Tanaka family was in the direct employ of the shogun and, when Nobunara learned Tommy was the sole survivor of the American Mission, took him under his protection. Events later indicated it would be embarrassing for Tommy to be presented to Perry when the commodore returned the next year. Instead, Tanaka had a most unusual proposition for the boy: The samu-

2

rai and his principal wife, Joshi, were childless—he offered to adopt the young American, if Tommy agreed.

The lad did and, for the next twenty years, he trained in and lived the life of a samurai, going into service for the shogun. As to his obligation to the U.S. Navy, Tommy took care of that not long after his fifteenth birthday, when an American legation was officially established in Tokyo (Edo).

Tommy presented himself and resigned his warrant, thus squaring himself with the navy. The penurious administration, responsive to a strong antimilitary climate among the voters, required him to forfeit all back pay due him. Tom believed the bargain worth it.

The years passed and the War Between the States intervened. Tom Fletcher lost all contact with his native land. Then, through the Japanese legation in Washington, a letter was delivered to Tom—now known as Tanaka Ichimara Tomi of the Fujika *rentai* samurai, Master of Horse and Standard Bearer to the Shogun. The letter came from Tomlinson, now a general in the Union Army. He had chosen his allegiance to his country over that of his state and had risen in the ranks during the recent war. The general's message wrought changes in Tom Fletcher's life. Tom's two elder brothers had given their lives fighting heroically, but uselessly, for the cause of the South. Not in itself an unusually tragic thing; so many had fallen that the massive numbers made individual sacrifices insignificant. But the news General Tomlinson gave next drastically altered his future. The Fletcher plantation, along with that of the Tomlinson family—despite their open Union sympathies —had been razed by Yankee troops.

Those responsible were known as the Bummers. They started out as legal detachments, authorized to loot and pillage as a part of Sherman's "Scorched Earth" policy. That authority came from Sherman's infamous General Order 13, which also decreed that blacks captured in Confederate uniform would be summarily hanged. In the case of the Bummers, some of the more zealous went even further. To protect Sherman

3

from any possible repercussions, many a wise adjutant listed such men—and units—as AWOL. In particular, the officers and some enlisted men of a certain regiment; the 251st Ohio, were believed responsible for the massacre and pillage of the Fletcher plantation.

Worse news followed. Tom's father had been beaten, tortured, and hanged. His mother and sister were raped repeatedly and then butchered with a sabre. A younger brother, one Tom had never seen, had been decapitated by a single sword stroke. Their livestock had been driven off, crops burned and their few slaves cast out to fend for themselves and all the buildings burned to the ground. Uncaring, the raiders had ridden off with their loot.

Proper soldiers during the day, at night, many men of the 251st Ohio were suspected by Sherman's headquarters of becoming marauders, committing the most outrageous atrocities under the direction of their own commander, Colonel Edward Hollister, a wealthy Ohio merchant who had raised and outfitted the unit in Cleveland and brought them to war. Nothing was ever proven, but the names of those suspected of complicity were known to General Tomlinson. Would Tom Fletcher be interested?

Under the code of *Bushido*, the Japanese warrior's creed, which Tanaka Tom Fletcher had followed for more years than his own Western culture, he was duty bound to avenge this crime against his family and property. He in fact had no other choice, save *seppuku*, the ritual suicide of a samurai who has failed. Arrangements were made and the samurai, Tanaka Ichimara Tomi, sailed with Japanese diplomats on their way to Washington. There, investigation revealed that Hollister was believed to have kept about him many of his partners in crime, operating like a feudal lord on the frontier.

Since learning this, the vengeance bound samurai had ridden against Hollister's gang, or parts of it, on three occasions. In the first instance, he had come face to face with the evil colonel himself, only to be compelled to

4

watch helplessly as Hollister escaped into Mexico. Hollister, Tanaka Tom was coming to learn, had more in mind than merely operating a large gang of outlaws, made up of the riff raff and scum of both sides in the war. Tom was as yet to discover the true extent of Hollister's ambition, but it seemed the man, protected by layers of respectability and political influence, had a dirty finger in nearly every criminal activity west of Dodge City.

At the Ancha Mesa Apache reservation, Tanaka Tom managed to seriously hamper Hollister's financing scheme. Gold had been discovered on the lands of the Valbajo Apache band. One of Hollister's men plotted to get it. Tanaka Tom stepped in the way. The results were fatal to Hollister's dream of easy riches in Arizona.

Later, in San Francisco, an Occidental-Oriental clash that threatened to unleash a race war turned out to be only one of the symptoms, not the disease. Buried under the gold-and-red lacquered facade of Chinatown, an ancient evil—the Tongs—flourished and through them a sex-slave ring that Hollister hoped would ultimately fill his coffers. The flashing *katana* and blazing revolver of the Six-gun Samurai brought doom and destruction to the Tong and the ambitions of a corrupt politician who supervised the scheme devised by the tainted colonel. Where Tom Fletcher might strike next depended upon the list provided to him by General Tomlinson. When he did, it would be with speed and strength.

Tom Fletcher was a big man, even among the Occidentals of his time, standing an inch over six feet, broad shouldered and narrow in the waist. Westerners, accustomed to a diet of meat and potatoes, considered him skinny, weighing a spare 165 pounds, for all his size. His straight black hair and matching dark eyes, with a slight almond shape, and high, Oriental cheekbones, he had inherited from his mother. As had been the case with many early settlers in the colonies of Virginia, the Carolinas, and Georgia, several of the Waverlies—his mother's family—had married into the "almost white"

Cherokee Nation. That heritage had manifested itself most noticeably in Tom. His older brothers and younger sister favored his yellow-haired English father. Tom's years of rigorous training as a samurai had toughened and conditioned his body until not a motion or gesture was wasted. He moved with the silent, ominous grace of a tiger and could pounce as quickly and fatally. He rarely smiled and the furrowing of his dark brow carried with it the icy feel of death.

His vices were few and moderate; his dedication to *Bushido* and his quest absolute. He ate sparingly, preferring *cha* (tea), *gohan* (rice) and *sushi* (raw fish) to beefsteak. Women he considered a necessary, desirable, but expendable, part of any man's life. His morality was based upon the sharpness and accuracy of his *katana* (samurai sword), the swiftness and strength of his horse and the favor of his ancestors. He accepted life as it came to him along with the ever-present possibility of sudden, violent death, both of which he saw as mere aspects of his *karma* (preordained fate).

When Tanaka Tom Fletcher set foot on American soil after an absence of twenty years he was, in every way, the perfect killing machine.

Chapter One

Heat waves shimmered off the desert floor of Utah as the twelve-car train of the Kansas & Pacific began its ascent of the Rocky Mountain pass called Gunnison Gap. Smoke belched blackly from two tall, mushroom-like smokestacks, whose bell-shaped upper works ground sparks into harmless particles, as a pair of powerful locomotives chuffed loudly, laboring mightily to draw the string of passenger and freight conveyances up the steep incline into Colorado.

Sagebrush and scrub gradually gave way to pine trees, eliciting excited remarks from all those in the two chair-cars and pullman . . . all, save one, who sat in regal silence, body stiffly erect, poised on the edge of the horsehair padded, red plush velvet seat. A narrow vertical furrow between his dark eyebrows gave the only indication that he didn't particularly like travel by train.

This was, in fact, only the third trip by rail for Tanaka Tom Fletcher. The first had been from Washington, D.C. to the sprawling, sleepy town of Los Angeles, where he'd begun his quest. Later he had traveled, wounded and helpless, from San Diego to San Francisco, in the company of Wei Chang and his daughter, Mei Lai, aboard a Southern Pacific cattle car. He liked that even less and now, after three long, uncomfortable, sooty days from San Francisco to here—changing from the Southern Pacific in Salt Lake City to the southern route of the Kansas & Pacific—he was even more uncertain of its advantages. Though the pride and arrogance of a samurai, bred so deeply into him, prevented him from any greater show of discomfort. Tethered in a stock car, far forward by the engine, were his Morgan stallion and pack mule. Tom wondered if it wouldn't have been wiser to have sacrificed speed for that more familiar mode of travel. Yet he had an important meeting ahead of him in Colorado.

Some buried instinct told him that he must keep that appointment at his earliest possible opportunity, or lose contact with one of the men he sought. Bradley Ashton had served as a lieutenant in the 251st Ohio, under Colonel Edward Hollister. Hollister had left San Francisco a few days before, using this same train route, headed perhaps for Colorado. The only clue Tom had to Ashton's whereabouts was a notation on his list: *Last known to be in vicinity of the mining camp at Cripple Creek, Colorado.*

While waiting for his own train, Tanaka Tom had questioned men pointed out to him as having recently come from the Colorado gold fields. From them he learned that a man answering to the name of Ashton was supposed to be establishing a religious community in a mountain valley some distance west of Cripple Creek. Such news frequently came amidst snickers and snorts of derisive laughter. One old hard-rock miner summed it up for Tanaka Tom.

"If'n you're a friend of that loco preacher from New Caanaland, Mister, I can plain out say you pick some mighty strange pards."

Encouraged by this malediction, Tanaka Tom set aside pursuit of Hollister to deal with this isolated irritant, Ashton, spurred on by the knowledge that since Hollister had been headed this way, he could well be with his former lieutenant. Tom's thoughts on the subject were interrupted by the entrance of a white-coated concessionaire.

"Coffee, folks! Hot coffee! San'wiches. Fresh ham, or head cheese, or Chicago loaf on home-baked bread.

Enjoy 'em while they're fresh. How about you, sir? What'll you have?"

Tom Fletcher turned a bland, impassive face to the food merchant. "Do you have some tea? A little rice, perhaps?"

The concessionaire started to frame a sarcastic reply, but his eyes took in the steel-hard muscles and taut expression of the big man before him and he changed his mind. "Hmmm. Don't recollect ever bein' asked for them things before. If I would have, I'd sure have 'em."

"Then you will be carrying them in the future?" Tom's question came in a hard, flat tone that brooked no disagreement. The thin whisps of samurai moustache drooping around his thinner lips gave added grimness.

"Aaah . . . er . . . hmmm." The salesman turned away abruptly, a light sheen of sweat breaking out to gloss his nearly bald head. Tanaka Tom permitted himself the smallest of satisfied smiles. Of all the bad traits of mankind, a samurai learned to hate hypocrisy the most.

The encounter had amused him, though, provided a distraction from the boredom of the trip. How then could he spend the remainder of his ride? Relax, think pleasant thoughts of peaceful gardens, each stone and plant placed precisely in the one optimum spot to enhance the beauty and "rightness" of all the others. A harmony of color and texture, the construction of formal gardens had long been practiced in Japan until it became an art form. Such serenity, apparently, was utterly unknown in this rushing, bustling Western world. Or should he look at the passing scenery? Absorb it so that he could compose a *haiku*? Aaah. That's it.

> *Snowy pines slipping by,*
> *Grandeur of barren rock here.*
> *Life comes dying.*

He would remember that one. Perhaps build on it, taking part of the thought, making a new poem, as in *haiku* contests among samurai of the same *butai*. His sensitive ears picked out the distant shriek of wheels on iron rails, slipping as they lost traction on the steepest part of the grade. Then came the sussurant sibilance of sand pouring onto the rails from the bunkers. The keening of metal on metal changed pitch. The cars lurched forward as the locomotives regained purchase on the slippery track. He should see to his horse, Tom thought. He could calm the dark Morgan and flighty mule, prepare them since their arrival in Grand Junction couldn't be far off now. And he could take his *hibachi* from the pack, heat charcoal to prepare a meal. He rose from his seat, intending to make his way forward to the stock car. Suddenly movement outside the window caught his eye.

Five men rode from among the trees, half-hidden in a swirl of dust as they spurred their mounts to close with the creeping train. Each rider held a weapon in his hand—pistol or rifle. Their faces were masked by gaudily colored bandannas drawn up over their noses. As Tom watched, a spurt of gray-white smoke formed at the muzzle of the leader's gun, followed by a sharp report. The other men began firing their weapons. Glass shattered in a window part-way down the car and a woman screamed. Tanaka Tom alone calmly accepted that this was a holdup.

"The Larcher gang!" a man near the front of the car shouted in a trembling voice.

Tom Fletcher turned back to his seat, reaching into the webbed, hammock-like compartment strung from the ceiling and retrieved a long, highly ornamented and lacquered case, sliding it smoothly into the left side of a wide, decorated sash that spanned his middle. Next he checked the Colt's Model 1871 Single Action that rested in a low-slung holster on his left leg. This suited his natural left-handedness, and tradition demanded that the *katana* be used primarily as a right-handed weapon. As he completed his preparations, the bandits reached the train. They separated with military precision, each to his assigned duty. From the direction of

10

the engines, a gunshot sounded, followed by an agonized cry of pain. Another revolver discharged, another scream. Steam hissed and the train jolted to a stop.

Doors at each end of the car opened and two masked men entered, revolvers drawn.

"All right, folks. Everyone stay where you are, dig deep and dump it into this bag," the one facing Tanaka Tom announced forcefully. He released a handful of gathered burlap, opened the yawning mouth of the sack. As he advanced down the aisle, he encouraged the reluctant with a waggle of his gun muzzle. At the third rank of paired seats, he met open resistance.

"I'll thank you to keep your filthy hands off my brooch, young man," a gray-haired dowager with an enormous pouter pigeon chest declared as the outlaw reached for a diamond pin attached to the velvet lapel of her coat.

"Lady, this is a train robbery. You cough up like everyone else. Now give!" He snatched out, jerking roughly on the jeweled pin, tearing it from the cloth.

The angered matron acted unexpectedly fast for a person of her age. She drew a long hat pin from the drooping velvet millinery creation that topped her head and struck with violence, burying it deeply in the back of the outlaw's hand. He yelped in surprised pain and lashed out with his revolver. The barrel struck the woman in the side of her head, tender skin tearing easily and blood flying.

When the stickup man raked his .44-40 Remington downward the high front sight caught in a fold of flesh at the corner of the woman's eye. Her soft, aged skin parted and ripped freely, exposing the eyeball and tearing further until a jagged rent disfigured her cheek all the way to her jawline. Scarlet gore flew in every direction and a woman across the aisle screamed her way into hysterics. Undeterred, the train robber reached down and plucked a small purse from his unconscious victim's fur muff. When he looked up he saw Tanaka Tom advancing toward him.

"You were told to stay put, Mister. Now heel!" The

11

outlaw swung his long-barreled Remington toward Tom's broad chest. Then a slender ribbon of bright light seemed to appear at the end of Tanaka Tom's hand. Accompanied by the rasping hiss of metal on lacquered wood, it whipped out and upward in an *iai* lightning draw.

The keen edge of the *katana* sliced through the gunman's elbow, letting the amputated member thud to the floorboards still holding the firearm firmly in whitening fingers. The robber stared in horror at the thing that had once been a living part of him. Then a scream erupted, loud and penetrating, as his terror overwhelmed him.

Tanaka Tom completed his stroke, rolled his wrist to reverse the samurai sword's edge and swung back while taking a short step to the right and pivoting on the balls of his feet. Then, with both hands on the haft of the sword, he used the momentum of his body to deliver a *yokomen* side-head stroke.

The blow silenced the man's scream as Tom neatly struck the robber's head from his shoulders. The body did a grim parody of running in place while being inundated with a shower of blood, blasted ceilingward from the severed carotid arteries by his pumping heart. All the while the gory rain splattered on the passengers, evoking more cries of terror. Then the message reached the rest of Jim Larcher's being and the corpse fell in a heap.

All in the same instant, Tanaka Tom executed the next right-lead step of his technique, which took him past the dead man, pivoted ninety degrees left so that a bullet whistled harmlessly through the space he'd formerly occupied. His left hand withdrew two slender, dart like objects from his *obi* while a belated warning shout got by a second blast from the other outlaw's revolver. The noise added speed to Tom's movements as he whipped back his arm and threw the poison-tipped *tonki* at the other train robber.

The slivers of steel caught the man in his throat and upper chest. The sticky black substance that coated

12

each needle tip came from a decoction of the leaves of certain plants—the process of their preparation known only to the Master Armorer of each samurai *rentai*. The poison so derived attacked the nervous system, so that almost immediately the outlaw went into convulsions and fell to the floor of the train, while Tanaka Tom advanced on him, drawing his Colt .45 and finishing the writhing man.

Two more women began to scream, along with a sissified drummer, traveling with a line of ladies' hats. His long, slender, pallid fingers stroked nervously at his ashen cheek and he rolled his eyes upward, slumping into a faint. Tanaka Tom glanced that way and curled his lips contemptuously. In three strides he reached the open door and left the car.

A quick look right and left showed Tom the other robbers, gathered near the closed door of the mail car. Two of them blazed away at the windows while the third, under their covering fire, ran forward to attach bundled sticks of blasting powder to the unmoving barrier. Tanaka Tom, Peacemaker in his left hand, samurai *katana* raised high in the other, charged toward them. He filled his lungs to their greatest and released his battle cry.

"K-i-i-i-a-y-y-y-i-i!"

Startled, the three men looked up. Their jaws sagged at the sight of the strange apparition descending upon them and belatedly they realized that the unorthodox weapon the charging man held was only a variation on the more familiar scythe of Old Man Death. In their frozen moment of hesitation, Tanaka Tom dashed in among them.

Tom's *katana* flashed overhead, then fell in a *shomen-uchi* cut. A .44-40 cartridge discharged deafeningly near his ear, the bullet wounding only clear mountain air as it plowed skyward. The hand that held the Remington revolver was attached to the far end of an arm that was no longer attached to anything. Seemingly unaffected by the loss of one arm, the outlaw who previously owned it tried to draw a wide, thick-bladed

13

bowie knife from his belt. As he did, the *katana* swung to the right, then back left in a horizontal stroke.

A great burning pain, like a hot brand being drawn across his belly, flashed through the man and he suddenly sat down, his remaining hand trying to stuff purple-yellow coils of intestine back into the gaping wound in his abdomen. He heard a solid plop beside him and glanced down to see his saddle partner, Norvie Blake, staring up at him from the ground.

Only Norvie still stood behind him, a quick look assured Deke Larcher, trying to swing his Henry carbine into line with the rapidly moving man who had attacked them. His mind swimming in pain, Deke tried to figure out how this could be. His sudden hot, sticky baptism in Norvie's blood gave him a needed clue.

The outlaw leader began to scream, realizing that the big man had cut off Norvie's head. Deke continued to shriek his horror for several seconds, until he died from his own blood loss. As his body toppled to the grass, the blasting powder went off.

Caught by surprise, the sole remaining outlaw had forgotten to move away from the mail car after placing the explosive charge. The blast tore the upper half of his body from the lower part, hurling it several feet away. His muscles, though, tried to carry out the last command of his brain. He completed his draw and fired a shot harmlessly into the turf, some twenty feet from where Tom Fletcher stood, his weapons at rest. While the sound of the explosion echoed through the mountains, Tom crossed leisurely to the mail car.

He looked inside, curiously, seeking to learn the effectiveness of explosives as an instrument of war. What he saw convinced him of the benefit. The mail clerk and guard had been shredded by flying slivers of wood and metal. Acrid smoke hung in the battered carriage and the undamaged walls were slippery with a coat of blood. Tom Fletcher turned with a shrug and hurried to the stock carrier.

He rolled open the door and dropped the ramp. Inside Tanaka Tom saddled his Morgan stallion, slipped a

14

halter on the pack mule and led them, one at a time, from the railroad car. He cleaned his smeared sword on a dead man's shirt and resheathed it, then swung into the saddle. Drumming the heels of his soft brown samurai boots into the stallion's ribs, he rode quickly away. Behind him he left a growing cluster of goggling, open-mouthed spectators.

Half an hour later, two hard-bitten men, one of them leading a pack mule, approached the train from behind. They reined in and sat their mounts, silently examining the scene while the conductor rushed to them.

"Holdup! They killed both engineers and a fireman and blew open the mail car. It was the Larcher gang. Can you fellers go for some help?"

"Why d'n't ya just drive the train on up?"

"I'm just a conductor, Mister. I don't know how to run a locomotive. We've got some hurt folks here. Will you please ride ahead to the division point in Grand Junction and have 'em send back a relief crew? The railroad will reward you for your time."

"Reward?" asked the one who had spoken first. A new light of interest glowed in his eyes. A hint of smile played about his dirty lips, giving his unshaven face mobility. He tugged at one scraggly end of his tobacco juice-stained moustache. "There any reward for this Larcher gang?"

"Sure there is. But there ain't no more Larcher gang. You've never seen the likes. There was this feller among the passengers, great big guy. He took after them with a long, funny lookin' sword. Cut 'em to pieces, he did. Got Delphus Olsen and Jim Larcher first, then went after Deke Larcher and Norville Blake. He didn't have to do for Con Murphy—powder blast on the mail car tore him in half.

"Then this feller off-loads his horse and outfit and rides out. I tell you, it was a wonder to behold."

At the mention of a big man with a sword, the riders exchanged meaningful glances. When the conductor came to the end of his recitation, the tobacco-chewer spoke again. "Hmmm. What do you say, Clive? Looks like another crime to add to the list. He must have killed his partners and took off with all the loot."

"Fits, Travis. Let's make tracks."

Travis McNee restrained his partner with his voice. "We're claimin' the reward on the Larcher gang, Mister Conductor. And when we catch up to that sword swingin' galoot that was ridin' with them, we'll bring him in the same way. You tell the railroad agent to have the sheriff make out that reward to Travis McNee and Clive Niebocker."

The conductor swallowed with difficulty, trying to lubricate a suddenly dry throat. He recognized, if not the names, the breed . . . *bounty hunters*.

"Yes, sir, Mr. McNee. I'll do that, yes, sir."

Chapter Two

"There you are, Mister. Five hundred dollars, dead or alive for the Larcher gang." The sheriff shoved back in his battered old swivel chair, patting his spreading middle. He looked across his desk in his office in Grand Junction, Colorado, at the tall man before him.

"Ain't often we pay a bounty man without he brings in the prisoners or their bodies. But the telegraph operator down at the railroad verifies all you said. When the Eastbound went on the board as late, they sent an engine out to look for it. A boy went along with a key. Just a few minutes ago he sent back word that sure enough the Larcher bunch had tried to rob the train and they all died the way you told it." The sheriff winced at the thought. His loquaciousness ended suddenly. "Messy way of doin' it, usin' a pig sticker like that."

Tanaka Tom Fletcher frowned at the sheriff's choice of words. "A *katana*, Sheriff. The traditional Japanese samurai sword. Hardly what one would use to stick pigs."

Sheriff Hastings waved a careless hand, dismissing the serious tone the conversation had taken. He licked his lips as Tanaka Tom counted the gold coins and put them into a pocket of his Levis. "Just a figure of speech, Mister. No offense meant."

"And none taken, Sheriff. I have . . . been out of the country for a long while, but I'm learning. Thank

17

you for the reward money. It will help me considerably. Good day."

"Good day to you, sir." Hastings breathed a sigh of relief as the broad-shouldered, dangerous-looking man walked out the door. He poured himself a cup of coffee, noticing that his hand shook slightly as he spooned sugar into the gritty brew. *A sword, for God's sake!*

Tom Fletcher headed directly to the livery to reclaim his Morgan and the stolid, gray mule that hauled his modest outfit. He'd learned long ago about the benefit of claiming reward money. It had happened in Nevada. On his way to seek one of Edward Hollister's gangs, he had come upon a stage holdup.

Acting quickly, Tanaka Tom had killed two outlaws and subdued the others. When he brought three cadavers into the nearest town, a small reward had been paid out. A strange custom, he thought at the time, but he was grateful for it. He accepted as his *karma* that, on those occasions when he could obtain it, bounty money would help in his mission of vengeance against Colonel Hollister. Now, satisfied with the ease with which the train robbery incident had been settled, he made ready to move on toward his meeting with Bradley Ashton.

"What do you mean you've already paid out the bounty money on the Larcher gang!" Travis McNee demanded in an angry voice.

"That's what I said, feller. Man name of Fletcher, Tom Fletcher, came in here yesterday, long toward evening. His story checked out, so I paid up. End of case."

"Sheriff, you made yourself one mighty big mistake. Here . . . look at this." McNee drew from his vest pocket a grimy, much creased square of paper and unfolded it. He thrust it angrily toward Sheriff Hastings. "See here. Fletcher is wanted in San Francisco for three murders and arson. One of those killings was of a police officer, Lieutenant O'Neal. We're all lawmen here and I know how you must feel about that. We've been on his trail for a long time. Figgers to us he was in with

18

the Larcher crew on this train job. Sort of an inside man, if you know what I mean."

"You can forget that, boys," Hastings replied calmly. "Railroad says nothin' was taken, the passengers even got back their money and things. No. He weren't with the Larcher bunch."

"I figger different." McNee's tone was cold, unrelenting.

"Hell, man, he had those people helpless. Couple of them that saw him use that sword of his'n up and dirtied their drawers. He had any part in that robbery, he'd have taken all the loot. Only figures. Now, if you've no other business with this office, why don't you ride on? We got little use for . . . *your* kind in Grand Junction."

McNee's eyes narrowed, his face flushed with anger. "That a threat, Sheriff?"

"No. Only a good piece of advice. My deputy . . ." As he spoke, from behind the bounty hunters the rabbit-ear hammers of a double 10-gauge cranked noisily back to the full-cock position. ". . . is right behind you, anxiously awaiting the pleasure of escorting you *gentlemen* to the city limits. I'd be obliged if you didn't keep him tarrying too long. Afternoon to you."

McNee blanched, but tried to cover his fear with bluster. "We're goin', Sheriff. But you'll see us again . . . to collect this here reward on Fletcher. He's as good as dead meat right now."

"Figures. Scum like you don't often transport a man back for trial. Now get out of my office!"

McNee dropped his bold front when they reached the boardwalk. He kicked angrily at a dirt clod that had been thrown onto the walk by a passing wagon. In dark silence, escorted by the vigilant deputy, he and Niebocker stomped down the street to the livery. Their horses were waiting, already saddled. The unspeaking deputy eased himself onto his own mount and urged the men on their way with the ominous black muzzles of the shotgun.

Once outside the growing community of Grand Junc-

19

tion, the badge left them. McNee looked after him with a dark scowl. Clive Niebocker reined in with a surly growl.

"Fine fix, you ask me. We lose the re-ward *and* Fletcher. You got any idee where to look for him?"

"No. But wherever he's gone, we'll find him."

NEW CAANALAND—GOD'S COMMUNITY
5 MILES
STRANGER TURN BACK LEST YE BE SAVED

Tanaka Tom Fletcher sat his Morgan stallion at a "Y" in the road, studying the sign. The right branch led to the town of Aspen Gap. Off to the left lay Bradley Ashton's community. The sign verified his informants intimation of it being a religious community. Tanaka Tom thought of this while he contemplated the fork in the trail. Which way to go first? Right or left . . . dexter or sinister? Fletcher smiled briefly at the aptness of that choice. He eased the plaited rice straw-traveling hat of a samurai back on his well-formed head and felt trickles of sweat run down his forehead toward his thick brows. Why not ride on in?

Ashton wouldn't know him. The former Union lieutenant probably wouldn't even recognize the name if Tom gave him his real one. He could be in, settle the score, and ride out, leaving behind another headless corpse, before anyone could realize what had happened. Easy. Then his training as a samurai asserted itself.

Do not engage an entrenched enemy without first seeking to determine his strengths and weaknesses. A maxim of Murukai, his first *butaicho*—his detachment commander—in the Fujika *rentai*, a man who had become a close personal friend. *To attack an unknown force is for the hare to place himself willingly in the hunter's trap."* The words of his aged personal instructor in the Tanaka home, during his days of youth, came to him with alacrity. A smile quirked his lips, faded.

No. He would not place himself in the hunter's snare,

20

as Murukai had warned against. Not when he could easily avoid any disadvantages. He would ride in a ways, then abandon the trail, skirt the valley, and spy out the land, making note of the people, their habits, occupations and defensive capabilities. Touching heels to the Morgan, Tom reined the sleek stallion to the left.

Lying prone behind a screening line of brush, Tanaka Tom made careful note of the comings and goings of the men, women, and children of Bradley Ashton's New Caanaland. The men, most of whom looked like farmers, wore somber black or brown coats and trousers, flat, dome-crowned "pilgrim" hats and scuffed boots. Long, square-trimmed beards covered the lower part of their faces.

The women dressed in voluminous, shapeless dresses of unrelieved plainness. Not a ruffle or bow disturbed the bland sameness of their costumes. Equally drab, oversized bonnets covered their hair and masked their features. A few younger ones wore what looked like a Catholic nun's habit, done in white. The children wore miniature versions of their parents' unimaginative garb. Tom Fletcher had been at his observations for three hours now and several things besides this struck him as especially odd.

No sounds of music or gaiety came from the village. None of the women sang as they went about their tasks, neither the men nor the children whistled snatches of some tune to lighten the day's work. And he heard no laughter. No shouts of glee came from the youngsters and none broke into spontaneous play. In fact, everyone seemed to move about as though in a trance. The enthrallment was most noticeable in the smaller boys and girls.

At noontime they had formed in ranks in the village square, before what must be the church, and marched in regimented silence to a building Tanaka Tom figured to be their schoolhouse. None of the usual playground paraphernalia adorned the bleak, barren ground around the unpainted structure the children entered. From time to time the measured chanting of young voices came from the open windows, unrelieved by anything of a light-hearted nature. Tanaka Tom moved his eyes away from the dolorous house of learning, making note of the other things he found strange.

A lazy column of dust rose in the air, following a man who worked a plow behind a harnessed team of mules. As he toiled, he looked neither left nor right and, despite the heat of mid-day, he had not removed his dark woolen coat. No canteen or clay water jug rested in the scant shade of the split-rail fence that described the farmer's field. Nor, though rabbits scampered in profusion from the path of the plowman, did the farmer have along a rifle to bring down such easy game for the pot. Tanaka Tom arrested his gaze while he tried to recall if any of the people he'd observed that day had been armed. His memory told him they had not.

To verify this most unusual of situations, Tanaka Tom took his Dolland, a compact, pocket-sized telescope, from his *obi*. The small, but powerful, brass-cased spy glass had been his first purchase when he returned to America. He had owned one during his midshipman days and admired its excellence. He drew it to its full extension and shifted positions to study the village.

A few moments scrutiny verified his earlier impression. Not a man carried a gun, not a rifle or revolver. No long arms, shotgun, or rifle, rested against the side of any house where the women worked in kitchen gardens or hung out clothes to dry. It was more than unusual, Tom reminded himself. Small bands of Indians still roamed this western part of Colorado Territory, and desperate men, down on their luck, willing to take any chance to build a stake. Self-protection was a rule of survival. Yet, not even a belt knife was in evidence on any resident of New Caanaland. No, Tom corrected himself, returning the glass to focus on a rugged looking man standing in the doorway of a low sod building, there was at least one man with a gun.

22

He wore it slung low in the manner of a seasoned gunfighter. Bright brass cartridge cases caught glinting shafts of sunlight as he changed position, leaning against the wooden door frame. His lips formed a cruel, hard line and a dull, drooping moustache obscured his upper lip. The grips of his Colt Peacemaker were worn smooth from much use and the handle of a large bowie knife showed on the other side, above the belt that held up his trousers. Tom Fletcher had seen his kind frequently since returning to his native country. Often such acquaintanceships had ended in violence. He swept the small village again.

There was another man with a gun. Seated on the porch of what must be the parsonage. Bradley Ashton's house. As Tom watched, another similarly armed man came from the interior of the building, and spoke to the lounger. He came erect and accompanied the messenger inside. What use would Ashton have for gunfighters? Tom stored the question for later and moved again. He spotted a fourth gunslinger-type out by a large field where a group of young, apparently unmarried girls worked.

Their backs were bent low, nimble fingers picking weeds from among rows of pale green vegetables. The plants looked familiar to Tom and he focused the telescope on them. Peyote! The Dream Cactus his Apache friends had told him of and had, no doubt, used in the rituals when he was adopted into the Valbajo band. What in the world would anyone be cultivating peyote for? Tanaka Tom's cogitation on a possible reason for this was interrupted by the mournful tolling of the church bell. Tom moved the glass to see what this would bring about.

At the field, the gunslinger, obviously a guard of some sort, shouted something to his charges. The girls dropped their work where they stood and listlessly walked to a stile over the split-rail fence. They formed into ranks, shoulders slumped and faces blank. At a command from their overseer, they began marching toward the village square. From the door of the school,

23

the children spilled out into the yard, taking places in a two column file. On their teacher's order, they, too, began to march to a place in front of the church. Three of them, Tom saw, appeared to be crying. A quick look around confirmed that everyone was leaving his work to converge on the central plaza. Puzzled, Tanaka Tom hadn't long to wait to learn the purpose.

A medium height, slender figure, his features hidden in the folds of a golden-colored cowled robe, stood in front of the open doors of the church. As he moved with stately tread down the steps, two more hardcases appeared in the doorway behind him. They held between them a small boy. Grasping him tightly, they also advanced.

The three men and their young prisoner halted before a wooden structure. Everyone had assembled by then, forming an open, three-sided box around the central square. When the bell stopped, absolute silence held over the assembly. The golden-robed man stepped forward and raised his arms in a benediction. His thin, reedy voice carried through the quiet to Tom Fletcher's ears and, as the man spoke, one of the gunfighters produced a knife and made a swift slash at the back of the boy's collarless shirt. He ripped the cloth and peeled it from the boy's body, letting it hang in shreds from the lad's tightly bound hands.

The small child could hardly be more than eleven or twelve, Tanaka Tom thought. Even by Japanese standards he was skinny, his ribs standing out starkly, knobby, protrusions at shoulders, elbows and hips. His gaunt frame pulled far back in a sweeping arch below his rib cage, yet his little stomach protruded roundly, showing the early effects of malnutrition. His mop of tow-colored hair and delicate, slight features made him look even younger. Caught again by the golden gowned man's words, Tanaka Tom listened in growing disbelief as the ritual scene played itself out.

"Jamie Dorn, you are accused by your sister, Margaret. She has sworn upon the Holy Book that last eventide, when you should have been in your house, on your knees, with your family, for vespers prayers, she located you behind your father's barn, in the act of befouling your body, *the temple of God's spirit*, with vile *meat*!

"You have sinned greatly, Jamie Dorn, for to take pleasure from the eating of flesh is doubly as deadly an evil as to take pleasure from all other things of this sinful world. Worse, to allow yourself to take a life to feed your body is a sin so black that the Almighty will turn his eye of favor from you until suitable penance is done. We of the Brotherhood of New Caanaland know that man is born in sin and will live and die in sin. Seeking forgiveness and salvation is the only path to righteousness. The punishment decreed for the evil act of eating the meat of animals is six lashes. Have you anything to say before sentence is carried out?"

Jamie Dorn pulled himself free from his wardens, walking proudly, head held high, toward the robed figure. Although Tanaka Tom could see the cold sweat of fear glistening on his naked chest. His thin, piping voice sounded clearly over the distance.

"It ain't right, Rev'rend Master. We're hungry all the time. We cain't sing or whistle. We cain't play. We cain't go fishin' or swimmin' or do nothin' but work and study and pray. We cain't do *anything* until we're old enough to have growed a beard." Jamie thrust his chin defiantly at the unseen features inside the cowl. "What kind of God is it that says a little boy cain't enjoy bein' alive? Cain't learn about things for hisself? Cain't even have enough to eat? That ain't fair!" He half turned, raising his bound hands in appeal to the congregation. "I ain't done nothin' wrong. Sure, I et meat an' I forgot it was time for vespers . . . didn't hear the bell. But . . . awh, it was only a little rabbit and I was so awful hungry."

Sudden revolt strengthened Jamie's voice when he realized he could not escape the punishment. "Besides, Margaret lied when she said I did it all the time . . . and that's a sin too. Why don't the Almighty want her punished too?"

25

"Blasphemy!" The gold-robed man recoiled as though bitten by a snake. He raised his arms again in supplication, his voice a soprano tremulo. "Oh, how evil is an unrepentant child! I pray the Almighty's mercy on His humble people. Forgive us, Lord, for nurturing so vile a serpent in our bosom." He turned an accusing finger and fiery words on the hapless boy. "Repent, Jamie Dorn. Fall on your knees and beg His forgiveness for the evil things you have said and done. For your blasphemy and sinful defiance of the ordinances of the Brotherhood, you shall suffer three more lashes. Foreswear your unrighteous ways before it is too late!"

Standing among a group of young girls who wore the habitlike gowns and head coverings, yet seeming separate from them, stood a tall teen-ager in a plain white, cowled robe. Sixteen-year-old Margaret Dorn compressed thin, bloodless lips to suppress a smile of wicked satisfaction. Her flat, watery-blue eyes glittered with malicious joy as she thought of what would come. She'd get even with Jamie, she exalted. She'd fix him once and for all. Black-hearted sinner, he'd get his now.

Tears ran down Jamie's face and his throat worked spasmodically before he could speak. His words, though, still sounded courageous defiance. "I got nothin' to be sorry for. The Lord didn't strike me dead with lightnin', like you said He would, when I went swimmin' buck-nekked, so do what you're gonna. It won't hurt."

"Anathema!" the cowled figure cried, making a mystical pass in the air. Then, calmed again, he ordered, "Let the punishment begin. Deacons, do your duty."

At the command, the two gunmen, named "deacons" by Ashley, came forward, grasped Jamie by his bare shoulders and hurried him to the whipping post. They released the cord that secured his hands and tried to lock him in a pair of manacles attached to the crossarm of the post. Jamie's thin wrists slipped through the holes. With a grunt of disgust, one deacon grabbed up the length of rope, cut it in half and used the two pieces to

26

secure the little boy to the whipping post. The task completed, the pair stepped away and another deacon, took their place. Jamie turned his head so that he could look at his tormentor. His skin, stretched tightly over protruding bones, trembled as he watched the man ripple the bunched muscles of his shoulders and arms and draw back a cat-o'-nine-tails. The blissful smile on the deacon's face clearly indicated how much he enjoyed his work. At a nod from the cowled figure of Ashton, another boy, about Jamie's age, marched to place beside the post and began a slow drum roll.

"Begin," Ashton commanded in a sepulchral voice. The lash whistled through the air.

Silence from the crowd when the knotted tips of the flail hit flesh. But a stifled gasp came from Bradley Ashton, who quickly thrust both of his arms deep into the double-sided pockets of his golden robe.

The second lash fell, breaking pale white skin on Jamie's back. Blood ran in thin ribbons. Bradley Ashton felt a growing tightness in his throat, a humming, vibrating excitement that coursed through his body, bringing a familiar pressure to his loins.

The third blow fell, rending more flesh, bringing a whimper from Jamie Dorn, despite his vow not to show pain. A convulsion shook the boy and Bradley Ashton at the same time. Ashton felt the urgent, swelling thrust of his manhood and the fingers of one hand stole in that direction.

"Stop it! For the love of God, stop it!" a woman cried out. A grim-faced man who stood next to her, his small stature, fair skin, and white-blond hair proclaiming him as Jamie's father, took her in his arms and pressed the woman's face to his chest to stifle her protests. At a nod from Ashton, the flogging continued.

For the fourth time the cat descended, throwing droplets of crimson in a welter from Jamie's ravaged back. Some of them spattered on the drumhead and the face of the boy beating it. Rivulets of sticky redness flowed down Jamie's skinny body, under the tightly belted trousers. A moan escaped Bradley Ashton's lips. In that instant he realized that this display only fired his erotic hunger. He would have to placate it by some means . . . and soon.

The fifth and sixth blows fell in quick order, sending fresh cascades of blood along the rivers that flowed over the boy's buttocks and along his bony shanks, to become visible again as they ran over his bare ankles and feet. Jamie arched his back and screamed in pain until he lost consciousness. One of the deacons picked up a bucket of water and hurled its contents onto the lad's back. When Jamie moaned and began to move again, Ashton nodded to the man with the whip.

The seventh lash cut into Jamie's back and again he shrieked in agony, writhing helplessly until, mercifully, he passed out once more. Ashton felt an exhilaration that brought him close to an involuntary climax, yet outwardly exhibited testy impatience as he curtly signaled to a deacon to sluice the boy down with another bucket of water. Jamie shuddered and revived with a groan, in time to scream again as the muscular deacon applied the cat for the eighth time.

"Oh, please, *please*!" Jamie's mother sobbed. "He's just a little boy."

"Courage, Sister Sally," Bradley Ashton admonished. "It is all according to the Lord's will and is being done for the good of his soul." The cowled head nodded for the final blow. Ashton started to say more about the evil the lad had done, but cut off his words with a strangled gasp as the ninth lash struck Jamie's mauled body.

The boy's ordeal ended with a shriek of agony that faded into pitiful whimpers. Ashton felt his body convulse and his unnatural nature ran its course, expelling moisture onto his trembling fingertips. He wiped his hand on the inside of his cloak. A smile illuminated his face. He knew now what he needed to quell the demon that burned within him. He turned toward Jamie, who hung slacky from the shackles of the whipping post.

"Jamie Dorn, you have sinned mightily and mightily have you paid for it. Let us pray that you go forth from this place of punishment to walk the paths of righteousness. For your days are numbered and the chances to repent are few and surely He keeps score." He turned back to the blank-faced people. "May the Almighty bless you and keep you through all your days and armor you against the weakness of sin. Before you depart, beloved brothers and sisters, it is my pleasant duty to announce that the Lord has revealed to me that the time has come to welcome another soul into the Sacred Sisterhood. The fortunate one, chosen by Him and shown to me in an inspired revelation, is . . . little sister Rachel Miller. All Glory to the Lord. Hallelujah!"

"Hallelujah!" the congregation repeated dully.

"The time chosen for our little sister Rachel's glorious initiation is tonight, following evening prayers. She is to come . . . alone . . . to the Holy Sanctuary and there be united with the Almighty. So be it."

As the crowd dispersed, they seemed more animated than before, almost jubilant. Faith made their faces bright with righteousness—the only form of pleasure they were allowed in New Caanaland. One thirteen-year-old child, though, Rachel Miller, stood alone, white-faced and shaken. Born of a knowledge few others possessed, she looked upon her upcoming "elevation" with horror and, like the Dorns for their young son, she was filled with revulsion.

Tanaka Tom withdrew from his observation point. He felt disgust and a lack of understanding for what he had witnessed. The cause came not from the punishment itself, for he came from a life and culture that countenanced far worse, rather his confusion resulted from the reason behind the flogging and the way in which it had been carried out.

First, although he could understand the purpose, his sympathy lay with the boy. He recalled his own gnawing hunger during those first days in Edo and how he would have literally killed, if necessary, to get something to eat. The lad had not stolen the food. And why, in this Western culture, was there a prohibition to eating meat? He thought of his own childhood days in Georgia. By the time he and his friends had reached the age of nine, they had all killed and roasted rabbits and other small game, playing wild Indian in the woods. Yet none of them had even suffered so much as a swat on the rump when caught.

Then, as the whipping progressed, Tom quickly recognized the obvious sexual excitement the act of flogging generated in the man he now accepted as Bradley Ashton. It made him think of the stories he had heard in the Tanaka household about a certain daimyo who derived pleasure out of tormenting low-born peasants unfortunate enough to fall into his hands. Although such excesses had been outlawed more than a century before that time, the vicious nobleman liked to watch while the adults were boiled alive . . . lowered a bit at a time into the bubbling water. Then he would relieve his lust on the tortured and broken bodies of young boys and girls. He had eventually been caught in the act by agents of the shogun and forced to commit *seppuku*. Yet Tom's Montalta and Valbajo Apache friends tortured in order to draw strength and power from their dying prisoners. Confusing. One thing, though, seemed obvious: When his time for retribution came, what he did to Bradley Ashton might indeed meet with the approval of more than one other person.

Chapter Three

Divested of his ceremonial robes, Bradley Ashton sat at his desk going over a large set of financial ledgers. He carefully perused the neat columns of figures inked onto the pages. A smile creased his smooth, almost boyish face as he came to the final entry under assets. Amazing how little space it took, he considered, pleased with himself, to represent a great deal of money. For a moment he let his thoughts wander back over the past, calling to mind his former commander in the Union Army.

Wonder how well Ed Hollister is doing? he mused. During the war the colonel of volunteers had put forth some grandiose plans. Ashton had been young then, of a prominent Cleveland family and a lieutenant in the 251st Ohio. The looting expeditions Ed Hollister had organized down in Georgia had been exciting and profitable. As the third son, Bradley Ashton stood to inherit little of his father's estate, so he availed himself of these opportunities to build a stake for after the war. Some of the excesses that Hollister and several of his men gloried in repelled young Ashton, but he grew callous enough to ingore the lesser of them and, on occasion, gloss over the remainder.

Hollister had offered him a position in his "Grand Design" when their spree of murder and looting ended at the sea and, a few months later, Lee met with Grant at Appomattox. Bradley Ashton declined. He cherished some ideas of his own on how to prosper after the war.

He had a second reason for refusing the colonel's offer, although he had been slow to realize it.

"You want your usual after-dinner brandy, Reverend Ashton?"

Bradley interrupted his thoughts of the past to reply. "No, Joe. That's all right. You may go now. Just close the door there, will you?" No drinking tonight, he reminded himself. He wanted all his senses sharp for the evening's activities. Relaxing in his padded swivel chair, he let his mind flow back over the years to the closing days of the Civil War.

His reluctance to join Hollister's enterprise, Bradley Ashton later realized, came from the fact that already the fires of religious zeal were flickering to life in his mind and body. Always sensitive as a child—a failing he readily acknowledged—he remained so as an adult. He found the over-abundant and unnecessary violence Hollister and his Bummers engaged in repulsive. Yet, after months of witnessing their indulgent acts, he found himself stirred in unexpected ways. Frequently he reached a pitch of sexual arousal, often achieving an orgasm before he could take his turn in the defilement of their victims. After so much time, the sex of the victims didn't affect his gratification either. In reflection, these things disturbed him. He spent many months, following the unit's disbanding in their native state, delving into any sources he could obtain on the subject. He read de Sade, the accounts of Gilles de Rais and others. All the while, he worked to set in motion his own plan for a comfortable future.

An unfortunate boating accident claimed the lives of his eldest brother and fiancée. This set in motion the heart of his scheme to aid his ambitions. Terrance, the middle Ashton brother, became the victim of an unusually cold winter. While out ice fishing he fell into the frigid Ohio River and thus expired.

A soft, diffident, knock interrupted his reflections. Frowning, he spoke pre-emptorily. "Yes? What is it?"

Joe opened the study door. "Larry Don's here, Reverend Ashton. Shall I have him wait?"

"Send him on in. There's coffee in the kitchen. I'll only be a few minutes longer." After dismissing the man, Bradley Ashton returned once more to those long ago days in Ohio, following his second brother's death.

For several days after the funeral, Bradley prayed and prayed, seeking a sign that God's will had been done in this striking down of both his brothers. Then, confident that God's designs and his own were the same, he had stealthily buried the axe with which he had weakened the ice his brother Terrance had stood upon, fishing. Tragedy seemed to stalk the Ashton family that year.

In the early spring, his father fell victim to something he ate. An error by servants in picking wild mushrooms was blamed, and Bradley inherited the family fortune. In short order, he departed for the West, leaving his mother well provided for.

Bradley Ashton thought fondly of the years that quickly came and went. In Omaha, Nebraska, he had attended a revival meeting—the result of an over-indulgence in John Barleycorn and an unexpected maudling sense of guilt over his recent actions regarding his family. It was funny, he reflected, how the absolutism of the fire-and-brimstone preacher had made him see things in a different light.

His eldest brother had been a fornicator. On two occasions he had personally come upon Michael and his fiancée in "compromising" circumstances. And Terry had been a liar and blasphemer . . . to say nothing of his preference for young, pre-pubescent boys. His father? Well, he had been a profiteer, hadn't he? His company made enormous wealth off the sufferings and death of millions of young men in the recent war. Emboldened by this revelation, Bradley sought out the evangelist, conferring with him long into the night on several occasions. When the week-long revival ended, Bradley Ashton left Omaha with him, a partner in the revival-faith-healer-dentist business.

Ashton looked up from the ledgers again as Larry Don Saggerty knocked softly and entered the room.

The rugged-looking gunslinger took a chair and sipped at his cup of scalding hot coffee. He knew better than to interrupt his boss and waited silently to be acknowledged. Ashton gave him a nod and turned back to his books, picking up the thread of his thoughts.

Two years later, during a periodical sweep through the gold fields of Colorado, Bradley had experienced the divine revelation that had inspired the eventual creation of his communal religious society in Yellow Creek Valley. His inspiration came from the astonishing contents of a thin volume published in London a few years earlier by a fellow named Karl Marx. Bradley and the evangelist parted ways and Bradley began stumping the camps, preaching his new brand of religion.

The concept didn't come to him full blown. He had worked on it, enlarging his plans and revising his doctrine until he developed the rules by which he would run his Utopian paradise. Odd, he mused, but as time went by he'd found himself more than half-believing the holy double-talk with which he bedazzled his gullible converts. Particularly within the last year or so. Always, though, in the back of his mind was the desire to amass great personal power.

Wealth and power. The figures before him showed that he had achieved both. His projections indicated that he could do even better. Bradley's reflections returned to Colonel Edward Hollister. How fared the colonel's fortunes? Not nearly so well as his own, Bradley thought smugly.

"Larry Don?" Bradley Ashton broke off his-reverie to return to business. "How are things going for our new convert families?"

"Ya mean them suckers in Aspen Gap waitin' to dump their money into the church's pocketbook?" Larry Don Saggerty had a way of getting right to the heart of things. He wasn't befuddled with the religious hokus-pokus of Ashton's "Holy City," despite his position as "Deacon of the High Altar." He knew what he really was; chief enforcer for his boss. It didn't matter to him if he took it away from some pilgrim with a gun or with honeyed words, the results were the same; *you* wound up with *their* gold. Of course, this way had its points. The pay was good and a guy stood less chance of gettin' shot up. Especially since the cult's laws prohibited ownership of guns to all but the deacons and the boss.

But lately the boss had seemed to be swallowing more and more of his own malarkey. Saggerty's native cunning warned him that he had better humor Ashton if he wanted to keep his cushy job . . . more to the point, since he'd seen some of Ashton's fits of rage, if he wanted to keep his life.

"Sorry, Rev'ren'. What I mean is, the Channing family has received their ill-got gains from the sale of their farm and are ready to enter New Caanaland on this next Sabbath. Ol' John Altman still ain't seen the light, but that good-lookin' young wife of his an' the kids is champin' at the bit."

"We must exercise charity when it comes to an unbeliever, Deacon Saggerty." Unctuous tones accompanied Ashton's frown of mild rebuke. A sudden, unholy light suffused his face and his eyes glowed with an infernal brightness. He quirked his lips in a superior smile. Larry Don Saggerty had seen this expression before and it always made him uncomfortable.

"Of course, a *widow* can always dispose of property as easily as the original landholder, can she not?"

"You're right, boss. I'll . . . ah, see to it if you want."

As abruptly as the spell had come upon him, it passed. Ashton raised a restraining hand. "No, let it rest a few days. They are coming to the sabbath service this Saturday, aren't they? The Altmans?" He checked a list of names, indicating outsiders who had received passes to enter the valley. "Yes. Here's their names. I'll wax exceedingly strong on the evils of money and how it can be purified only by sanctification in the church and through use for the common good. If that doesn't do it . . ." The mad glow returned.

"Then we shall see about other means. Now, I have

35

to make ready for the investiture of dear little Rachel." Bradley Ashton unconsciously smacked his lips in anticipation. "Leave me." As Saggerty departed, Ashton felt an expectant stirring in his loins.

Chapter Four

Only a single candle lighted the dirt-floored common room that served as kitchen and living space in the Miller dwelling in New Caanaland. The two loft areas of the sod house were given over to sleeping quarters for Peter and Alice Miller and their children. Tonight, though, no one slept there except Davey, the youngest child. Thirteen-year-old Rachel sat at the table, facing her parents, tears running down her cheeks, sobbing wildly, her older sister, Martha, trying to calm her, an arm around the slim little girl's shoulders.

"I c-can't, Daddy. I just *can't*! It's nasty what they have to do. I w-won't be a Sacred Sister . . . *I won't*!"

"Rachel, Rachel, how can you say these things? Why, the Reverend Master says we must all serve in the capacity the Almighty chooses for us. Surely you've let your imagination run away with you." Gray-haired Peter Miller had married late in life and fathered three children; two girls and a boy. He had become a convert to Ashton's new faith following a five day binge in Denver. After he spent the last of his nuggets from a played-out gold strike, his angry, disappointed wife had dragged him along to listen to a street-corner sermon of a fiery-eyed zealot. Peter Miller at first rejected the message of the Reverend Ashton, but his wife pressed her every advantage. At last he gave in. Repentant, nagged at for a month by his wife, he had disposed of all his material possessions and moved his family to

Yellow Creek Valley. A simple man, he left questions of faith and doctrine to his wife. In his present confusion he turned to her now.

"Your father's right, Rachel. You should be happy. Proud of the blessings that the Almighty has bestowed upon you."

Rachel's face contorted with real terror and her small fingers tore at strands of her auburn hair. "Oh, Mother, can't you see?" she pleaded. "It's not a blessing! It's *awful*. H-he . . . he m-makes the girls . . . do all kinds of d-d-dirty t-things . . . to him . . . to his . . . I won't! *I won't, I won't, I won't!*" The girl became hysterical.

Alice Miller, whose normal maternal protectiveness was smothered by self-righteous indignation, recoiled from her daughter, her face white with sanctimonious rage. Her hand lashed out, slapping the girl soundly on one cheek.

"How dare you say such things! The Reverend Master is a good man. Good . . . as in *God-like*. Do you hear me? How could you possibly say such evil things?"

Rachel gulped down the last of her sobs, replying in a hoarse voice to her mother's challenge. "B-because . . . K-Kathy told me. Oh!" Her eyes widened with shock. "I . . . she made me promise not to tell . . . but I . . . won't go through what she had to do. I'll die first!"

Peter Miller rose, climbed the stair to the loft. He gently shook the shoulder of his sleeping nine-year-old. "David. Son, wake up. Go to the Nelson's house and fetch Kathy here, right away."

"Yes, sir," the boy sleepily replied. He slipped into his trousers under the blankets, as he had been taught to do, donned his dark, plain-cut coat and round-top hat and climbed from the loft. He scurried barefoot from the cabin. Behind him, his mother's voice rose again in caustic self-righteousness.

"Shame on you, Rachel Miller. For shame! How dare you speak evil of the Reverend Master in this house? He saved your father from the evils of strong drink and made this family whole again. I don't know what madness infects the Nelson girl, but I've a mind that a sound whipping would drive this blasphemy from you, young miss."

Peter Miller, who had been listening with growing concern to his daughter's revelations, placed a hand on his wife's arm. His voice, though strained, was firm. "Now, Alice. Let it be for the time. We'll hear what Kathy has to say for herself and then decide."

Alice Miller, now fully fired with holy zeal, started to make a biting reply when a knock at the door interrupted further conversation. Peter rose to answer it.

He opened the thin wooden portal to reveal, not Kathy Nelson and his son, but James and Sally Dorn and their boy, Jamie. They seemed nervous. After a brief pause, James Dorn spoke in a deep bass.

"May . . . ah, may we come in?" Once seated around the table, he declined an offer of coffee and got right to the point. "We . . . we're leaving this place of evil. My son was flogged for nothing more simple and natural and harmless than trying to feed his starving body. By damnit, this time the man has gone too far!"

Alice Miller's face twisted with anguish, her eyes echoing confusion and grief. "Has everyone gone mad?"

"Hush, Alice. Let the man have his say. What about your daughter, Brother James?"

Casting an almost apologetic glance at Alice Miller, James Dorn went on. "Margaret will not go with us. She's entirely dedicated to that . . . that unnatural Sisterhood of his." Jim sighed, a look of helplessness on his face. He spread his hands in a gesture of supplication. "As to the rest of us . . . well, J-Jamie's barely able to travel. His back is a mass of torn flesh. But I'll be damned if we'll leave him to the tender mercies of that . . . madman."

"Brother James Dorn . . . you are the incarnation of Satan!" Alice cried, covering her eyes and shrinking away from the short, thick-shouldered man who stood now, clutching his hat, his ill ease apparent to all. In a fleeting second he mastered his flagging determination.

"Call me *Brother* no more. I am Jim. Jim Dorn, by the Grace of God a free man again. Did you . . . did you see what he was doing? Ashton, I mean. While he . . . licked his lips and watched my boy lashed half to death he was . . ." Jim Dorn leaned toward Peter Miller, whispering to save the women embarrassment. "He was abusing himself." Peter Miller's face grew stony, eyes glowing with anger, an emotion he'd not felt in three years, as the color drained from his cheeks.

Softly spoken, though they were, the words reached Alice Miller. She sprang from her chair, arms flailing wildly. "Liar! Heretic! *Get out of my house!*"

"Enough, Alice!" her husband thundered. "Restrain yourself or leave the room. I have . . ." he continued to the Dorns, his tone nearly apologetic. "For a long time I have had suspicions about the good reverend and the things we must do to follow his religion. Although I must confess my suspicions were not along those lines. What is it you want from us?"

"We heard from Jamie about Rachel's . . . reluctance to join the Sisterhood, if it ever came to her being selected. We are leaving this place as we said. My wife and I—we thought maybe you would like to send Rachel along with us. David, too. He's been swimming bare-skinned with Jamie and some of the other boys. After what happened today one of them is bound to talk out of fear. It'll mean the flogging post for your son."

"Fiends!" Alice erupted, shocked beyond belief. "Filthy minded heathen brats! Oh, David shall be punished according to the laws of the church, all right. I'll see to that."

"You'll do nothing of the sort," her husband commanded.

Alice started to make a hot reply. Her self-righteous tirade ended, though, when she saw the angry glare in Peter's eyes. She clapped a hand to her mouth.

Silence held for several long seconds. Then David

opened the door, startling all inside, bringing with him Kathy Nelson.

The girl looked around the room, momentarily confused. She wore the habitlike garb of a Sacred Sister and her eyes were large with wonder and fear. She had been granted only a two hour visit with her family and was already late in returning to the dormitory of the Sisterhood. She spotted Rachel at the opposite side of the table, noting her tear-stained face and understood immediately the cause for her summons.

"I—Brother Peter, Sister Alice, I don't know what Little Sister Rachel has told you, but the truth is even worse than anything I said to her. All of the . . . the other girls went through the same things." Her cheeks tinted crimson with shame as she went on, revealing what had happened at her own initiation. "He . . . he . . . after he made me remove all my clothing, he . . . took from me . . . that which . . . I'm supposed to . . . to hold dear for . . . m-m-my husband! But . . . but it didn't stop there. After that he made me do the most painful, awful things that . . . that I can't . . . I won't describe." Kathy choked and began to sob violently, covering her face with her trembling hands.

"You needn't torment yourself further, Kathy," Jim Dorn said sympathetically. "We understand far more than you realize. We're leaving here. Would you like to come?"

Kathy pulled free of his fatherly hand on her shoulder, eyes now wide with fear. "Oh, no. I daren't. He . . . he said if anyone heard . . . if I attempted to leave the Sisterhood or run away . . . my . . . my whole family would burn for it."

"Kathy, Kathy, he couldn't do a thing like that. No one would let him," Sally Dorn said kindly.

"Who'd stop him?" her husband growled. "There's not a gun among the lot of us and those hard-case deacons of his wouldn't hesitate a second to unholster theirs. Even against unarmed men. Damnit! We're losing

41

time. Now, Pete, do you understand why we came to you?"

"Yes . . . yes I do. Of course, someone must stay to try to rally some opposition to Ashton. And, if the threat applies to only those who have been inducted into the Sisterhood, well, I suppose we'd be safe enough. But Rachel . . . Rachel must leave. Yes. I see that."

"No!" Alice Miller came to her feet, nearly shrieking her defiance of her husband's decision. "Don't you see? You are the evil ones. The Reverend Master is good, his church is good. You are betrayed by Satan and all his wiles. It's . . . a conspiracy. These children have been taken in by the Devil. Kathy, Jamie, Davey . . . all of them possessed. But I'll fight the Dark One. I'll stop him. My daughter has been dedicated to the church and the glory of the Lord. She shall be a Sister! I'll destroy the Devil. I'll go to the Reverend Master and stop you! My daughter will leave this house only to embrace the church."

"She'll leave it now to escape this madness!" Pete Miller roared back at her.

"Over my dead body!"

Pete swung, short, hard and fast, his open palm connecting with his wife's cheek. She blanched, fingers strayed to her stinging face. A look of shocked wonder removed her wild rage.

"Not your dead body, my dear, but surely over your obedient one. You will do nothing to prevent our daughter's escape from this . . . this monstrous man." Pete paused, looked at Rachel. "Now, Rachel, make ready to leave. You, too, David."

"Yes, Father," the children chorused.

"I'll go with them, Father. They'll need someone who's family." The eighteen year old girl's face showed determination though her upper lip trembled slightly.

"A good idea, Martha. Go. But hurry. Hurry!"

A gibbous, orange moon rose part-way above the peaks to the east, washing the land with its harvest-time light. Tanaka Tom Fletcher crouched beside a small fire, stirring tea leaves into a pot of boiling water. He had withdrawn over the ridge separating Yellow Creek Valley and Ashton's New Caanaland from the road to Aspen Gap. He had dressed for evening in typical Japanese style; wearing a brown silk kimono with a delicate lotus pattern worked into the weave in white and gold thread. His feet were encased in white *tabi* slippers and he wore a pair of wooden *gehtas*. His two fighting swords, never far from him, were secured tightly to his left side by the wide band of an *obi* that matched his kimono. He covered the pot to let the tea steep, and leaned back against the bole of a large pine. He breathed deeply of the resin-scented air, enjoying it, thinking of the distant, fragrant mountains of Japan. With one hand he rubbed the bristly stubble beginning to grow on his shaved pate.

Maintaining the hair style of a samurai became difficult to the point of near impossibility under the conditions of the West and his bushido quest. One barber, blissfully unaware of how near death he came, had nicked Tom's scalp twice before the Six-gun Samurai bounded out of the chair with a Japanese curse and snatched up the razor to complete the task himself. Bound by a twenty-year custom, but not so tightly bound as a native Japanese, Tom would not think of changing, though he did find himself of late defending the traditional hairdo by force of will alone. Time would tell on that account, he reminded himself. When he decided the brew had worked long enough, he rose to pour himself a cup.

Tom's mind dwelled on the things he had observed that day. The presence of armed gunmen indicated that Ashton's religious community surely wasn't all it appeared to be. Why would a man who had supposedly "got religion" need the services of gunslingers? Unless, of course, New Caanaland was only a front for other things. He concluded that she should get a closer look before exacting vengeance on Bradley Ashton. Could Ashton be working in some manner for Edward Hollister? Most of the other men on the list he had encountered were. But what use could Hollister make of a crack-pot religious cult? With an effort, Tanaka Tom forced himself to put aside his speculations and think serene and peaceful thoughts while he sipped his strong green *cha.* He let his mind drift, trying to compose a *haiku* about pine trees and the moon, then he abruptly jerked back to his surroundings at the distant, muffled sound of a hoof striking rock. Setting aside his teacup, his right hand went to the handle of his *katana.*

Rachel and Martha Miller felt utterly exhausted. They had trudged along through the darkness, labored up a steep slope for what seemed to be hours. Now, even the downgrade didn't bring the expected relief. Martha thought of her brother. Davey's luck. He rode double with Jamie to ease the battered boy's journey. No sore feet for him.

Martha had argued the logic of going cross-country to intercept the Aspen Gap road rather than taking the longer, easier route by the trail out of New Caanaland. Rachel had agreed with her, her tightly controlled fear of falling into Ashton's hands urging her to make all possible haste. Still, Martha thought, there must be an easier way. In all her eighteen years she had never extended herself so. She shuffled on, her aching feet crying for a rest, and skirted a huge boulder that loomed in her path. She looked up from the trail and jerked to a sudden stop.

Martha's hand flew to her mouth to stifle the scream that rose in her throat. Her eyes opened wide, growing round with terror, as she beheld the ghostly apparition that blocked the way before her. A true giant of a man stood there, dressed in outlandish clothes, his arms raised high in the air, hands clutching the handle of a long, slightly curved sword. Moonlight glinted from the keen edge that seemed about to descend upon her helpless body.

Chapter Five

Before the strangled cry of terror could escape Martha's lips, Tanaka Tom checked the downward swing of his sword. Behind Martha he had recognized, hunched over the saddle of the horse Martha led, the slender form of the boy who'd been flogged that afternoon. Keeping his weapon unsheathed and at the ready, Tom whispered harshly to the fugitives.

"Quiet! I won't hurt you. I am a friend." He came down from the rock and the refugees from Ashton's mad paradise gathered around.

"Hold on there a minute, mister." Jim Dorn came surging forward, showing no concern for the potent danger that faced them. "Who are you and how do we know we can trust you?" His belligerent posture came more from ingrained concern as a father and husband than from any expectation that he'd receive a satisfactory answer.

"Pardon me. These are hardly the conditions under which the conventions of polite meetings can be carried out easily, yes? I am Tom Fletcher, called Tanaka Tom. I am a stranger to these parts. You are . . ." Tanaka Tom left his question open in the manner he'd often heard Western men invite answers from strangers.

"I'm Jim Dorn. This is my wife Sally, and our boy Jamie. These are the Miller girls, Martha and Rachel, and their little brother Davey."

"You are leaving the valley?"

Sudden suspicion made Jim Dorn guard his words. "Are you askin' us because you work for Ashton?"

Tanaka Tom grunted. "No. I do not work for that man. I . . . I saw your son flogged this afternoon. Is that the cause of your departure?"

"In part, yes. The man's insane. A dangerous madman."

"If you wish to escape detection it is well if we get away from here. I have a camp over the next swell. We can talk there."

At Tom's campsite, Jim Dorn, with Davey Miller's help, lifted Jamie down from the saddle and propped him against a tree. Tanaka Tom forestalled all conversation until he had built a small, dim fire and added water and tea leaves to the pot to brew them a hot drink. The night chill of the high mountains had settled in with a sharp bite. Once each person had a steaming cup in hand, Tom took up the conversation.

"Your son was whipped for eating food? Is this right?"

"Yes, Mister . . . uh, Fletcher."

Tom smiled. "Tell me, if what he did was wrong by the rules of this New Caanaland, can that be enough to make you give up your way of life?"

"You don't understand," Jim Dorn began to explain. "Something has gone wrong, very wrong here in New Caanaland. The Rev'rend Ashton, back before he became the Reverend Master, was a good man. He spoke direct to a feller's heart in a way that made you just know he had been a sinner too and had found the path to salvation. We . . . all of us came there of our own free will."

Tanaka Tom's eyes glowed with inner expectation. "It is the Reverend Ashton, then? Bradley Ashton?"

"Y-yes. Why do you ask?"

"I . . . have a certain matter to settle with Reverend Ashton. But tell me about your decision to leave."

"It weren't that Jamie stole any food, Mr. Fletcher. He trapped a rabbit and cooked it up to eat. Meat is forbidden to the people of New Caanaland. It was more for eatin' meat and missin' vespers that Jamie got whupped."

"Among my own people, the eating of meat is not yet a fully accepted practice."

"*Your* people?" Jim Dorn inquired, confused.

"*Sumimasen, dozo. Gomen nasai.* Excuse, please. I mean in the land of my adopted family. I have lived as a native in Japan for the past twenty years. So. Your son disobeyed. This is a bad thing. Children must learn to obey . . . sometimes without question."

"At the cost of having the flesh whipped from their bones, Mr. Fletcher?" Sally Dorn's anger flared.

Tanaka Tom remained unmoved. "I have seen far worse, for considerably lesser offenses. But go on."

"Our boy's just getting his growth spurt—he's constantly hungry—and the children are worked so hard in New Caanaland. When they aren't in school, they are out in the fields, dawn to dark." Sally Dorn brushed back a stray lock of hair, fought down tears that watered her eyes. "It's . . . the land hasn't been good for us here. Not since we came here. As a consequence, the few vegetables, grain, we grow goes to feed the adults. The children must make do on a bowl of cornmeal mush twice a day. It leaves them starving . . . I suppose we all are, truth to tell."

"And the cream is separated off what little milk our cows produce to make butter for the deacons and Ashton," Jim growled. "Watered skim milk and mush! Every kid there is gettin' bowlegged from pellagra."

"That not eatin' meat's a lot of bunk, too," Davey Miller chirped up in his soprano voice.

"Whatever do you mean, Davey?" Sally inquired.

"Maybe *we* don't get any, but that don't slow down ol' Rev'ren' Ashton none. I seen him eatin' away on a big ol' steak more'n once. That's true, ain't it, Jamie?"

"Well, son?" Jim Dorn asked.

"Yes, sir. Davey an' me, we looked in through his winder an' seen him eatin' meat lots of times."

"Why, that pious old fraud, that . . . that son of a bitch!" Jim Dorn exploded.

47

Sally Dorn blushed. "James, your language . . . and in front of the children, too."

"Brad Ashton is a hypocritical *son of a bitch*, Sally. These youngins know it as well as you and I do and I'm going to call him a son of a bitch any time I've a mind to."

Sally Dorn issued a startled gulp and sought to change the subject. "Then there's the Sacred Sisterhood. Our oldest, Margaret, is a member. She was taken in four years ago. We've only found out tonight that it is a dirty, filthy thing, yet Margaret seems to glory in it. She's . . . she's become almost as big a power in New Caanaland as Ashton himself."

Martha and Rachel joined in then, somewhat reluctantly, and, for the next half-hour, the refugees unburdened themselves on Tanaka Tom. At the end of that time, he held up a hand for quiet.

"All right. I can see now that Ashton's ways have not changed, not that it would matter to me if they had. You are right in seeking escape. I shall escort you to Aspen Gap, if it is your wish."

Their noisy assent threatened to end the night's peace.

Where is she? What's keeping the girl? Bradley Ashton paced before the altar inside his Church of New Caana in a frenzy of passion. His loins ached and his swollen manhood throbbed with the need of release. *What could be keeping Rachel so long?*

A loud, insistent knocking sounded on the tall, thick oaken doors. Hardly the timid, virginal summons he'd expected from Rachel Miller. Gasping with expectation, Ashton hurried to open the grand portals.

Instead of a trembling expectant, pubescent child, whom he anxiously looked forward to slowly raising to the heights of sexual excitement as he'd done with so many others, he found Rachel Miller's mother, Alice, on the stoop, along with Margaret Dorn, the girl he'd elevated to the post of Elder Sister to his band of tender young flesh.

"They're gone! They've fled!" the distraught woman cried. "They've taken my daughter, stolen her from her duty to the church and disappeared into the night."

"Who? What? What are you talking about, my dear Sister Alice?"

"Those wicked Dorns. They came, along with that imp of Satan they spawned, and stole away my girls and my dear little Davey. Blasphemers! Defilers! Heretics! You've got to stop them, Reverend Master. Stop them!"

"Calm down, Sister. Calm down. What is this all about?" Ashton asked Margaret, who stood cold and remote as she always appeared, except when she lay spread-legged and wetly ready on the silken sheets of his bed.

"Brother James and Sister Sally came to the Miller cabin tonight. They and their hell's brat son, my one-time brother, Jamie, with them. It seems that Rachel didn't properly appreciate the honor of joining our Sisterhood. She'd heard some . . . stories about it from Sister Katherine. I've already seen to her punishment. The Miller girls, however, and their little brother, went with Brother James and Sister Sally. Sister Alice here, much to her credit, came to the Sisterhood dormitory to tell me this."

"They're going to Aspen Gap, Reverend Master," Alice Miller supplied. "You must stop them! The Lord will never forgive me if Rachel doesn't do her duty to you and the church."

Bradley Ashton found his lust diminished to a hot, walnut-sized lump in his groin. He beamed, despite his raging fury, at Alice Miller and extended a hand in automatic benediction. "Don't fear, my dear Sister Alice. I will organize a search for them. The Almighty will be appeased! Go now. I have much work to do." When Alice Miller reluctantly departed, Ashton signed for Margaret to remain.

"That holier-than-thou bitch!" Margaret hissed, referring to Rachel, rather than the departed Sister Sally.

49

"That sanctimonious hypocrite. How dare my parents do something so despicable, and how dare Rachel try to escape us?"

"Take it easy, my dear," Ashton soothed, drawing her inside, one hand caressing the sixteen-year-old's round little bottom. "It's perfectly natural. Only to be expected of some. Not every girl of twelve or thirteen takes to it as naturally as you did. Now, do me a favor, send Larry Don Saggarty to me, will you?"

The moon, having risen early, had traveled well down in the sky, when Tanaka Tom broke camp and started out with the Dorn party for Aspen Gap. Jim Dorn estimated the time to be near one-thirty in the morning and Tom urged them to make all possible speed, calculating that they would be hard-pressed to make the small mining town by late afternoon. To facilitate this, Tom distributed the people among the available mounts.

Jim and Rachel took one horse. His wife Sally, rode with Jamie, Martha sat in front of Tom on the Morgan and Davey, over many loud protests from the put-upon animal, was aboard the pack mule. With Tanaka Tom in the lead, they headed downhill toward the Aspen Gap road. A lowering afterglow of moonlight illuminated a long stretch of the rutted trail a scant three hundred yards ahead when Tanaka Tom called a halt.

"What are we stopping now for?" Jim Dorn asked, a bit worried.

"Quiet," Tom commanded. "Listen."

A faint sound of hoofbeats carried on the night air—several riders, coming fast. Alarm showed on Jim's face, as he, too, correctly interpreted the meaning.

"Your friends from back there have come looking for you."

"What are we going to do, Mr. Fletcher?"

"We haven't much choice. We fight, naturally."

Jim looked at Tanaka Tom with growing consternation. "B-but the women and children. What about them?"

"If they can't fight, they must hide. Hurry, the men are nearly here." Tom gave swift, terse instructions, sending the others uphill and choosing to remain in the center of action. Before the Dorns departed, Tom drew his Henry rifle and handed it to Jim, who faded into the shadows of the tall pines. In less than two minutes, Ashton's makeshift posse reined up on the road.

"Well?" a querulous voice whined. "We've come this far and no sign of them. I say we turn back."

"Christ, Rudolph" Larry Don snapped. "The first time you have to earn your pay and you want to sit it out. They didn't take the road, or we'd have come on them by now. That means they cut across country." He studied the hillside, calculating, orienting himself in relation to Ashton's village on the far side. Larry Don turned his horse first one way then the other, lips pursed, brow furrowed. At last he reached a decision.

"This spot is about opposite the village. They'd probably take the shortest route. As I recollect there's an old deer run that prospectors used to use, leadin' up outta the valley and over the ridge. It ought to come out about here. It'd take longer goin' that way, but it accounts for our not catchin' up. We'll spread out, head uphill. Remember, Ashton wants them back alive. But he didn't say in what condition otherwise. Let's ride!"

Crouched in the bushes, Tanaka Tom waited while the posse wended its way among the rocks and trees, climbing toward him. One by one they passed Tom by until a single rider, the complaining Rudolph, remained. He drew even with Tom when the Samurai rose, the keen edge of his sword whistling through the air. Steel bit into flesh below Rudolph's rib cage, slicing the man in half. A shriek of agony issued from the toppled upper portion while his horse, bathed in blood, bolted. It lunged forward, trailing warm, moist coils of intestine, the lower half of Rudolph still firmly seated in the saddle.

The frightened animal smashed into two others in his panicked flight, caused them to rear and plunge, and nearly dislodged their riders. Tanaka Tom, six-gun in

51

his left hand, sword held high in his right, charged upward to the next man in line. At the last moment the gunslinger managed to control his horse and bring his gun into play.

Tanaka Tom's Colt roared and the big 255-grain slug smashed into the other man's chest; pulped bone and lung and drove the life from him. At the same moment, Jim Dorn opened up from above. Zinging bullets from the Henry broke limbs and screamed off rocks. A man cried out in pain. Tanaka Tom was pleased that Jim Dorn had summoned some old combat sense and moved to a different location between each pair of shots. The Six-gun Samurai automatically adjusted his own line of attack and moved in on a third victim.

"It's an ambush! My God, there must be a dozen of 'em!" one man cried in confused fright.

"Pull back!" Larry Don Saggerty ordered in a bull-throated roar. "Pull back! Let's get outta here."

In ten seconds the disorganized posse had crashed through the trees to the road and headed back toward the junction, spurs painfully digging into horse flesh. Tanaka Tom sent a pair of out-of-range revolver rounds after them to speed them on their way, then sat quietly, waiting for the others to join him. When they arrived, Tom made a quick check to determine that everyone had come through all right, redistributed the riders and, with Tom in the lead, they ambled the still nervous horses down to the road.

"Next stop, Aspen Gap," the Six-gun Samurai told them with what he hoped was a light tone of voice.

Thunder sounded ominously over the Rockies while Travis McNee and Clive Niebocker sat their mounts, feeling the exhaustion of their long ride. Dawn had come gray and chill, and the threatening storm did little to raise their spirits.

"We're still cuttin' his sign, Trav. I say we move on."

"Yeah, Clive, but he's done left the road. It all don't make sense what with that notice back at the junction."

52

"What's that got to do with it, Trav? You know I cain't make out writin' real good."

"Up ahead here is some sort of religious community, called New Caanaland. Don't figure a gunslinger like this Fletcher would be headed there."

"Him leavin' the trail says he ain't exactly headed that way, eh, Trav?"

"You're gettin' the point, pard. Although he could be up to doin' those good people some harm. Howsomever, I got a feelin' we're gettin' close. We'll have to move cautious-like from now on."

"Then we're goin' on?" Clive Niebocker brightened.

"Sure we are, Clive. Sure we are."

Half an hour later, the two bounty hunters lost Tanaka Tom Fletcher's tracks in a rugged field of boulders. After casting around fruitlessly for several minutes, Travis McNee called a halt.

"Might as well light here a spell. We can have a bite to eat and then start swinging circles until we cut his sign."

"Fine with me. My stomach's pressed clear back again' my spine and callin' out to see iffin my throat's cut."

McNee built a small, smokeless fire and put on a pot of coffee. While it boiled, Niebocker cut thick slices from a ripe-smelling slab of bacon that was going green around the edges. Travis McNee watched him and built a cigarette. He tucked the cloth bag of Bull Durham into a shirt pocket and deftly twirled the paper cylinder between thumb and forefinger, licking it shut. He snapped a match aflame with a dirty fingernail and touched it to the crimped end, took a deep, satisfying draw and exhaled while he studied his partner through the rising blue-white tendrils.

"You know, Clive? We been partners for over a year now and it just came to me I never asked you how you came to be a bounty man. How is that?"

Clive chuckled wickedly. "You might say it was all by accident. I was ridin' the Owlhoot down New Mexico way. There was this little price on my head and some wet-behind-the-ears yonker set out to collect it. He weren't much of a bounty hunter, so it was me finished him.

"Well, I decides, here's a good way to get shed of this wanted-poster thing. I rode in with him slung over my saddle, in my clothes and turned him over as me. Made myself fifty dollars. That was after the under-the-table split with the sheriff. I took me off to a saloon to celebrate and got to thinkin'. Well, now, I says, this is an easier way of makin' money than robbin' banks. I reckoned to give it a try an' I been at it ever since. What about you?"

"My old lady got me into it."

"What?"

"My wife. The creek dried up and we lost all the stock, no money in the bank and no way I'd turn sodbuster for a livin'. The woman couldn't abide my lazin' around the house and I couldn't hold with her constant naggin'. So I saddle up one day and lit a shuck. First town I came to it was either go to jail as a vagrant or join in a posse out after some stage robbers. The stage company gave the posse a hundred dollars each reward. Then I did me some serious thinkin'. I'd tracked down reservation jumpers for the army oncet. 'Twas easy. An' the pay for bounty collectin' was mighty good, compared to a hand's wages. An' that was all I was fit for, me with a family to care for. So I gave it a whirl, liked it, and stayed with it."

"Yer family, eh? Ain't none of my business an' all, but is they the ones you always telegraphing money to when we claims a bounty?"

"The same. I love my wife though I ain't seen her in three years. She's a proud, good-lookin' woman for all her hard-workin' days. Got me two sons that'd make any man puff up like a horned toad with pride. Reg'lar scrappers they is, blond like their maw, big like me. An' a sweet li'l daughter, Carrie, that makes me pleased as punch."

54

"Aawh . . . hell . . . don't go gettin' sentimental on me, Trav. We got a job of work to do."

McNee shied a pebble off Niebocker's boot and reached for another when the sky above them opened up. The thunder and lightning had increased in volume and grew closer in interval while they talked, drawing nearer all the time. Now the heavens parted and poured down sheets of water. The tiny campfire hissed out in a billow of steam and the men dove for cover.

"There goes that danged trail!" Clive shouted over the roar. "We'll play hell findin' him now!"

Ten minutes later the storm had moved on and the emerging sun decorated the eastern sky with a rainbow. Trav and Clive tightened their saddle girths and rode out, swinging in wide half-circles off the original line of Tanaka Tom's trail. They crossed the ridge and began downslope toward the distant buildings of Brad Ashton's community.

"We might as leave ride on in and ask the Bible Thumpers if our man came this way," McNee suggested.

"No harm done," Clive agreed.

Two hundred yards down the road, three armed men stepped out of the brush and halted them. Caught by surprise, Travis and Clive stared helplessly at the gunslingers and back at each other.

"Just hand over them irons, boys," Larry Don Saggerty ordered.

"We come here peaceable, mister. We're law officers searching for a wanted man." McNee and Niebocker produced San Francisco Marshal's Office badges, given them by the clerk of the court along with the warrant for Tom Fletcher's arrest.

"Don't matter none," Larry Don drawled. A glint of cynical humor lighted his eyes. "You're in God's country now and it's Him that makes the rules. Now y'all shuck them irons and come along to the Rev'ren' Master. He'll decide what's to be done with y'all."

* * *

55

Sheets of driving rain fell out of the sky, obscuring the road ahead and instantly soaking everyone to the skin. Tanaka Tom Fletcher called a halt. He signaled the others forward and they anxiously gathered around him.

"We'd better find shelter," Tom advised. "We can't fight a storm this powerful." Violent gusts of icy wind blasted them, as if to emphasize the wisdom of Tanaka Tom's decision.

"Ground can't take all this, way it's coming down," Jim Dorn opined. "That means the creek'll rise. Might take out the bridge outside Aspen Gap."

"There you go again, James Dorn, borrowing trouble."

"Ain't no such a thing, Sally. It's only thinkin' all things through so's to be warned ahead of time no matter what happens. It's like ownin' a gun and never needin' it bein' a whole lot better than needin' one and not havin' it."

Tanaka Tom flickered a hint of smile. "We have a similar saying in the wisdom of *Bushido*. 'It is indeed wise to walk the forest path with *katana* at hand, even when no man threatens.' "

The cold wind and rain had revived Jamie Dorn. He sat up now and pointed one thin arm in the direction of Aspen Gap. "There's a little cave about half a mile up the road there. A sort of overhang thing. Can we make it there?"

"If you can lead us, Jamie," the Six-gun Samurai answered, smiling.

Chapter Six

Bradley Ashton looked up from the plate of stew he had been savoring as Larry Don led two strangers into the parsonage dining room.

"Who you got there, Larry Don?"

"Couple of drifters, Rev'ren'. We caught 'em out on the east road. Claim to be law officers. Bounty hunters more likely," the chief gunslinger observed.

"Well, well. Bounty hunters, eh? Names?"

Travis McNee noticed the unholy glow of madness in Ashton's eyes and decided to cooperate. "Travis McNee. And we really are officers of the court in San Francisco. We're hunting down a man wanted for three murders and arson."

"Bounty hunters," Ashton confirmed rightly. Early during his years on the frontier he had become familiar with the thin veneer of legality some courts used to cloak man stalkers. "Why, then, if you seek a criminal, did you enter this holy community?"

"The feller's name is Fletcher . . . Tom Fletcher. We trailed his horse this way until that storm last night washed out the tracks."

"There's no one here in New Caanaland named Fletcher. We are a peaceful, God-fearing congregation, working and singing praises to the Lord. No criminals in our midst."

This hombre had to be crazy . . . or a crook himself, McNee thought, his patience running out. "Cut the

57

crap, Preacher. You wouldn't be out here in the middle of nowhere if you weren't up to somethin' funny."

Ashton inclined his head slightly, his voice holding a bored edge. "Larry Don."

Larry Don Saggerty clubbed Travis McNee from behind with the barrel of his Colt. Staggered, the powerfully built bounty hunter turned to meet his attacker. A lump of well-polished brass glinted golden in the sunlight streaming into the room and Larry Don's knuckle duster collided with McNee's chin. Travis's eyes rolled up in his head, he gave out a lonely little sigh and slumped to the floor. Saggerty kicked him in the ribs for good measure.

"You don't talk disrespectful to the Rev'ren' Master, ya hear?"

"That's enough, Larry Don. Now, sir. Since you seem to be the only one remaining conscious in this partnership, perhaps you can be reasoned with."

"Yessir! Oh, you bet, Reverend sir. M'name's Niebocker. W-what is it you want?" Niebocker bleated.

"You, Mr. Niebocker, and this moronic lump-of-muscle out of my valley. Larry Don, bring in their outfits and let's make sure they are what they say they are."

"Right, boss," Saggerty replied, dropping any pretense at holiness.

In two minutes he returned with the saddlebags and bedrolls of the bounty hunters. He opened McNee's first. Upending the leather pouches, he dumped their contents on the dinner table. A carefully tied parcel of the newfangled commode paper bounded lightly into Ashton's stew plate, to soak up the juices. Saggerty repeated the act for Niebocker's outfit.

"Well, it's for sure they ain't no federal coppers, Rev'ren' Ashton. You want the boys should kick their butts outta the valley?"

"Rather coarse, Larry Don, but that I do. I do indeed." He turned again to Niebocker. "Now, Mr. Niebocker, I want it clearly understood that men of your ilk are not welcome in my New Caanaland. We are

58

building a paradise on earth here, all working equally, all sharing equally. You will each be fined one hundred dollars . . . or suffer a flogging at the whipping post. Then you shall be expelled from the valley. *Regulators*," Ashton made the word sound like a handful of excrement, "as your kind are wont to call yourselves in this part of the country, are a bane on human existence. Godless, blasphemous, drunkards, and users of tobacco, they are a thoroughly demonic spawn. Yellow Creek Valley, which I have renamed New Caanaland, is a closed community. Only the godly have a place here. Evildoers shy away from the shining light of the good. You and your thrice-damned partner here are no better than the men you hunt down. Leave here and never return, save through the healing grace of repentance and prayer."

An unhealthy light of zealous madness burned in Ashton's eyes. He rose from the table, one hand raised in benediction. "Amen, amen, I say unto you. Go forth and serve the Lord in the ways of righteousness . . . or suffer the wrath . . . ." He continued to babble on, oblivious of when Larry Don led Niebocker and the groggily recovered Travis McNee from the room.

Mud still mired down the slippery, narrow road as Tanaka Tom and his charges topped the final rise and looked over the town of Aspen Gap. The sun hung low in the West, where billows of white turned angry gray-green and black on their bottoms and formed anvil-headed thunder clouds over the snow-trimmed peaks of the Rockies. Below, in the valley, Aspen Gap didn't present much as towns go, but Tanaka Tom realized that the shelter it offered beat being caught in another downpour.

"Going to rain again," the taciturn samurai observed. "We'd better be riding on into town."

Grunting their protests, the weary mounts set legs stiffly against the slithering descent of the greasy track. The pack mule, unbalanced by his additional burden of Davey Miller aboard, floundered in his hindquarters and, once he broke free of the sucking mud, bounded across a grassy meadow, crow-hopping and twisting in an attempt to free himself from his clumsy cargo. Tanaka Tom smiled a secret, knowing smile as he observed the young boy, rather than screaming in fear, clamping down with his knees and staying with his fractious mount, whipping the round-topped, flat-brim "pilgrim" hat from his head and waving it in the air.

"Yaahooo! Yaaahooo!" Davey cried while he stayed with the mule, punishing it with the solid iron of the bit and hard leather heels of his shoes, at last forcing it back under control. "Hey! I'm a bronc buster," he cried shrilly as he walked the exhausted animal back to the others.

"Davey Miller, you should be ashamed of yourself," Sally Dorn scolded. "You could break every bone in your body showing off like that. You'll be the death of your mother."

"Leave him be, Sally," Jim Dorn intervened. "He's just bein' a boy . . . a whole boy . . . for the first time since his family moved to that hellhole. Besides, who's going to tell his mother? *We're* not."

Sally lowered her eyes. "Yes, Mr. Dorn."

Fifteen minutes later Tanaka Tom Fletcher and his band of refugees clumped over a wooden bridge and into the streets of Aspen Gap. A pair of old-timers, bearded and wearing only suspendered trousers over their age-grayed longjohns, eyed them with the transient curiosity of the elderly as they trotted past. A few chickens scurried out of the way and a fancily dressed city man, a gambler on his way to his night's work in a local saloon, tipped his hat to Sally Dorn and the girls when they paraded by. That comprised their welcome to Aspen Gap. Jim Dorn reined his horse to one side and stopped in front of the Denver-Santa Fe stageline office.

"We figure to be leavin' for Denver on tomorrow afternoon's stage. Might as well get the tickets now," the senior Dorn advised.

"Paw? Paw? Can Davey come along with us?" Jamie

sat erect in front of Rachel now. "I'd admire havin' a little brother and . . . and until his folks gets free of New Caanaland, he don't rightly have a family of his own. Huh, Paw, huh?"

Jim Dorn frowned. "I didn't bring you up to whine and beg, boy. You got somethin' to ask, you come right out with it like a man."

"Please, sir, can I?" Davey joined in. "Jamie an' me is best of friends. We . . . we get along right handsome and like the same things to eat an' all. Why, we fish together an' swim together an' never quarrel or fuss."

"Yes, *swim* together. We'll take up your bare-hided adventures at a later date," Jim Dorn announced sternly.

"We will at a later . . . Does that mean he can be my brother, Paw? Does it?"

Jim Dorn couldn't hold back a grin that brightened his face and softened the glower in his eyes. "For a while, son. Yes, for a while. Now, Mr. Fletcher," Jim turned to Tom. "I want to express our gratitude for all your help. We are all beholden to you."

"My honor would let me do no less. But I thank you for your kindness. Now I will see the Miller girls to a boarding house and take my leave. *Konnichiwa no sayonara*—good afternoon and good-bye."

"He's a funny feller, ain't he, Paw?" Jamie observed after Tanaka Tom rode away with the Miller girls.

"Watch your manners, son. I've a feeling that there goes more man than any ten of Reverend Ashton's gun-slinging deacons. We're lucky he sided with us."

Travis McNee's fury over his besting by Larry Don Saggerty held him in morose silence as he and Clive Niebocker rode out of New Caanaland. He stolidly rebuffed Clive's every attempt at conversation with a surly grunt, kneeing his mount ahead and locking his eyes on the ground in a hopeless attempt to locate any trail sign of Tanaka Tom Fletcher. Their unproductive task continued into late afternoon. Abruptly McNee reined in, his arm flung out, finger quivering in excitement as it pointed to the muddy verge of the road.

"There," he broke his hours-long silence. "See that arrahead flaw in the left fore-shoe? That's him all right." McNee studied the countryside in long, sweeping glances. Spotting the cave he grunted in satisfaction. "Must have sheltered from the storm in that there cave."

"What about all these other horses that joined in with him?"

"Don't know and don't really care. Clive, onliest thing that means is we'll have to be a might bit more careful when we go to close in on this Fletcher feller."

"The tracks lead toward town. What do you reckon we oughta do?"

"Wouldn't do to stumble into him all unexpected like. From what they said around the police house, he's faster'n a fresh-cut gilt with that dang sword o' his and meaner than a cornered wildcat. I figure we might just as well make camp and scout out the territory a bit tomorrow before we try to gather him in."

Clive giggled fitfully. "Shoot him in the back and collect the re-ward. That cain't come any too soon for me."

"Call me Maw Tamblin," the ample-breasted, roundly plump woman standing on the doorstep bellowed out in a full, rich voice that remained warm and mellow despite its volume. She stood with her pudgy hands on her mounded hips, surveying the two Miller girls and the strange-looking man behind them. Sure is a funny hairdo he's got. Wonder if he's one of those religious loonies over Yeller Creek-way? she thought, examining Tanaka Tom.

Her own gray-shot black hair was done up in a huge bun on the top of her head, as round and chubby as her pink-scrubbed, beaming face. Her twinkling black eyes didn't miss a detail as she inspected the trio. Her pink, rosebud of a lower lip curled disapprovingly as she took in the six-gun, slung low on Tom's left hip. And those sticks he wore in that fancy sash. Kind of sissified if you asked a body's opinion. With a start she realized that they must be swords. Now what would a feller be needin' with a six-gun and *two* swords? Mighty peculiar . . . but, a customer was a customer. She moved her roly-poly bulk aside, presenting them with the open door to her entrance hall and parlor.

"Come on in. No need to be jawin' on the outside, I always say. Neighbors learn your business fast enough without it. Come in, come in." Maw Tamblin preceded them into the parlor and indicated chairs. Once seated, she got right down to business.

"Now, my rules are simple. No men visitors in your room after sundown, and when they're inside during proper hours, always keep the door open. No strong drink, tobacco-chewin' or smokin', and rent paid in advance. Now you, Rachel, and you, too, Martha. Being sisters, I don't suppose as how you'd mind sharing one room? On account of I'm sorta squeezed tight for space right now. Rent will be, ah . . . umm . . . say, eight dollars a week since they's two of you. That includes board as well. You may use the tub once a week, set your schedule with the other girls. There's a sun-heated shower out in the wash house if you've a mind to be cleanin' up more'n that. Haul your own water. Well, what do you say, girls?"

"I . . . uh . . . that is . . . we . . ." Rachel caught the frown from her sister and cut off her words, waiting for Martha to take the lead.

"It's just fine, Mrs. Tamblin . . . Maw. We'll take it."

"You won't regret it, girls. I have only the finest young ladies living here. Won't have no truck with soiled doves or dancehall bawds." She grinned when she saw the blushes that colored both girls' cheeks. "An' another thing, no coarse language. I ask that all my girls maintain a ladylike manner at all times. Now, you sir," she turned to Tanaka Tom.

"Do you have any, ah, proprietary interest in these young ladies?"

63

"If you mean are they *jorō-musume*, no. They are not mine and they definitely aren't prostitutes. I, uh, came upon them on the trail. They told me their plight and I offered to escort their party into town. My obligation ends here at the house they will find shelter in. I bid you all a good day." Tom rose, started for the door on cat-footed tread.

"Not so fast, mister. You're no kin to them? No friend of long standing? You find them on the road and bring them here and now you think you can simply dump two defenseless children on big-hearted old Maw Tamblin and scoot out the door like a thief in the night? Ha! Think again. Your name?"

Tom fought hard to keep from laughing. Maw Tamblin reminded him of Aji-*san,* wife of the Tanaka steward. She, too, was bossy and officious, but easy to get around. "My name is Fletcher, ma'am. Tom Fletcher. Would you prefer I took them to my quarters over the saloon?"

Maw Tamblin's mouth gaped. "Heaven forbid! You seem a nice enough young man, Mr. Fletcher. You say you came upon them. What sort of difficulties were they experiencing?"

"They . . ." Tom hesitated, the natural suspicious nature of a samurai—bordering on paranoia—making him hesitant to say too much.

"We were escaping from that horrid Reverend Ashton over at New Caanaland," Martha supplied smoothly.

"Oh, really? Runaways, is it? I've heard rumors about that place—You'll have to tell me all about it sometime. Very well, Mr. Fletcher. Do you intend to stay around our town long? I ask because I have no wish to see these poor dears become indigent. They will need some sort of . . . ah, sponsor for easing their way over the rough spots in town."

"I won't be here long. I have a score of my own to settle with Bradley Ashton."

Maw Tamblin studied the grim features of the Sixgun Samurai, seeing death hovering there. "I see. Well, then, for a few days at least, can you help me get these girls introduced to life in Aspen Gap?"

"It would be my pleasure."

"Do let us know where you're staying then, Mr. Fletcher," Martha added. "And thank you so much for your help and protection." Tom nodded his acceptance and continued on to the door. He quirked his lips into a brief smile as he heard Maw Tamblin going on behind him.

"Now, girls, you are going to have to tell me simply *everything* about that Reverend Ashton and what goes on out there."

"I asked you to come, Sheriff, so you could hear this with your own ears. It's fiendish, it's . . . it's diabolical what that evil man is doing out there in Yellow Creek Valley." Maw Tamblin, her two-hundred-pound bulk agitated to the point of poising on the edge of her chair as though ready for flight, confronted Sheriff Harvey Wellman, holding back her flow of words with a visible effort of compressed lips.

"Well, then, go on with it. What is it you girls have to say?" Unconscious of his actions, the sheriff placed one hand on the paunchy bulge of his plain-front white shirt, while the other toyed idly with one down-turned corner of his walrus moustache.

Sheriff Wellman expected to learn of punishments like strappings, being locked in closets and other stringencies counted as horrid by females of tender years. What he heard, of sadistic floggings and tortures, told with cold fury by Martha Miller, left him gape-mouthed, his gray eyes clouded with anger. He swelled his chest, straining the buttons of his black vest, until his middle-age pot no longer protruded. When Martha's dialogue ended, though, he sat back, mopping his face with a large bandanna.

"You're certainly going to do something about it, aren't you, Harvey?"

"To tell you the truth, Arvada my dear, I'm not sure there's anything I can do."

Maw Tamblin shot backward in her chair, a hand fluttering to her pale cheek. "What are you talking about?"

"This is a religion, is it not? It's best for a lawman not to try tampering with folks' beliefs. Now I agree this man has gone a bit too far with his ways of punishment. But the Constitution says a man is free to believe what he wants and to practice his religion in the way he chooses. Since the rules of his religion are the laws of Ashton's community, there's simply no way I can put a halt to it."

"H-how can you say such a thing, Harvey?"

"I'm not sure if I can threaten him or even talk to him about it. Besides which, New Caanaland is in the unincorporated part of the Territory and I don't have jurisdiction. We'd have to send for a U.S. Marshall."

"Tell him about the other things, dear," Maw Tamblin encouraged.

Blushingly, Martha told Sheriff Wellman that Ashton frequently had his way with the young girls of the Sacred Sisterhood and also some of the younger boys of New Caanaland. "There is more," she concluded. "But modesty and propriety hold against my revealing the sordid details to a . . . ah, gentleman, Sheriff."

The Sheriff's long, horsey face grew red with anger and affronted morality, eyes glittering with suppressed fury. "That does it! By God, I *will* send for a marshal. Thank you, ladies. I know this has been a strain, Miss Miller, a trying ordeal. But I appreciate you bringing it to my attention. Something will be done, rest assured of that. Good day, now."

Not entirely satisfied with the Sheriff's response, Arvada Tamblin decided to take matters into her own ample hands. After Wellman's departure, she summoned several community leaders and gave them her own highly colored version of the goings-on at Yellow Creek. Her well-meaning, but overly dramatic rendition eventually drove an embarrassed Martha Miller from the room. Upstairs, in the quarters she shared with her sister, she settled herself on the bed and watched Rachel try to conquer the intricacies of knitting.

"Oh, darn it!" Rachel declared as she ripped out a stitch. "I was supposed to purl, not knit. What's got you looking so funny? " she fired at her eldest sister.

"Oh . . . nothing. Well . . . yes, I suppose there is. He's so handsome, don't you think?"

"Who? Mr. Dorn?"

"No, stupid. Mr. Fletcher . . . Tom. Tom," she repeated with a sigh. "Rachel, now don't you dare tell this to a living soul, but . . . I . . . think I have a crush on Tom."

"Now you're the one who's stupid," Rachel snapped.

Chapter Seven

Latigo Crowell had worked for Brad Ashton for a little over two years. He'd actually come there because of Larry Don Saggerty. Latigo rode with Saggerty and a couple of others in the past, robbing a few stages, mixing into an occasional range war, always skirting the fringes of the big time but seeing himself and his companions as true long-riders. This new set-up Larry Don had written him about had turned out good. The work wasn't hard, the pay better than average, and no risks. Late at night, they often talked together about letting Ashton grow fat on gold, then taking it all for themselves and riding out.

A good plan, Latigo Crowell thought as he stalked along the boardwalk of Aspen Gap's main street. But Ashton was no fool. A shrewd, greedy man, no matter he was half-crazy with this religion rot, who could act with all the ruthlessness of a madman. They'd have to wait and see what developed. Latigo turned in at the Denver-Santa Fe stage office.

"I'm lookin' for a friend of mine. Might have been through this way in the last day or so. Name's Dorn, Jim Dorn," Latigo told the clerk.

"Oh, yes, the Dorns. Whole family left this afternoon on the stage for Denver. Too bad you missed them."

"You can say that again, mister. Thank you anyway." Latigo left the office, a deep frown creasing his brow. Ashton would have a fit over this. Did those

Miller girls go with the Dorns? Larry Don and Ashton would want to know. He'd better find out.

"Couple of the prettiest little gals a feller ever laid eyes on, if they're the ones you mean," a loafer outside the Pot o' Gold saloon told Latigo Crowell twenty minutes later.

"That could be them. Sisters, they is."

"That they were," the idler affirmed. "Hear tell they're stayin' over on Murdock at Maw Tamblin's boarding house for young ladies."

"Well, well. Do tell. How do I find this place?"

"Just go around the corner here and down to the first street, turn left and it's a big ol' white barny place in the middle of the second block."

"Thanks, pard. I'll buy you a drink for your help."

"Obliged, son. Much obliged. Now?"

Latigo thought a moment. It would mean an all night ride to return to Yellow Creek, no matter when he left. That would be enough to give any man a powerful thirst. Might as well fortify himself. "Sure. Let's go on in."

Sunrise placed halos of pink, orange, and purple around the snow-capped peaks to the east of Yellow Creek Valley while Latigo Crowell descended the last three miles of road into the sleeping village. He felt exhausted and his winded mount had barely stamina enough to keep on its feet. Latigo's eyes burned and felt scraped raw, his throat parched and aching. He gave the blown animal its head until they reached the central square. There he reined in at the parsonage. Slip-tying his horse to the hitch-rail, he mounted the steps to the front porch.

Approaching hoofbeats had awakened Brad Ashton. He lay a moment, gaining full consciousness, then reached out, languidly, and stroked the firm, silken flesh of Margaret Dorn's delightfully rounded buttocks. Remembering the extensive repertoire of pleasures they'd given each other through most of the night brought a swelling to his loins. Sudden, loud knocking interrupted his erotic thoughts. Damn, he'd have to answer it and that would bring an end to their fun.

Ashton climbed from the bed. He slipped on a pair of trousers and padded, barefoot, to the door. "What the hell is it, Larry Don? Can't it wait until a decent hour?"

"No, sir. Latigo's back from Aspen Gap. The Dorns got away on the stage, but those Miller girls are stayin' right there in town."

"What! That little shit of a brother of mine got away?" Margaret's voice rose in pitch to a shrewish screech. She bounded out of bed and rushed to Ashton's side, taking no account of her nakedness as she threw wide the door. Latigo Crowell's eyes bugged and he felt a surge of blood to his groin, remembering the two exciting incidents when this alabaster-skinned girl had shared her favors with him. Larry Don Saggerty took in the display, one he often witnessed, with stolid indifference.

"How could you let that happen? How?"

"Now, Mag . . . uh, Elder Sister," Latigo defended himself, deciding that use of her title might calm the anger of this sixteen-year-old virago. "It couldn't be helped. The stage had done left by the time I got to Aspen Gap. The Miller girls are at Maw Tamblin's place, though. Bein' a hostel for young ladies, they sent Davey along with the Dorns, too."

"You're sure, though, absolutely sure, that Jamie is on his way to Denver?"

"Feller at the stage office told me he hepped load 'em aboard himself."

"Damn! Oh, damnit! How could he escape me like this?" Her anger turned on Ashton. "How could that *Almighty* of yours let it happen?"

"Don't think He had much to do with it, ma'am. They was all-fired anxious to get away, don't you know?" Latigo's flippancy earned him a black, hateful look from Margaret.

"Take it easy, my dear," Ashton soothed as he returned from the bedside and slipped a sheer silken wrapper over the naked girl's shoulders. "I never could understand your obsession with punishing Jamie."

Perhaps he couldn't understand it, Margaret thought angrily, but she knew only too well. For four long, marvelous years she had been the center of her parent's attention, a delight and joy to her father and comfort to her mother. She enjoyed a position somewhat unique among most children her age—an only child being a rarity—until . . . until Jamie had been born. The son her father had always wanted, Jamie took her place, as she saw it, in her father's affections. It was Jamie this and Jamie that and what a stout, sturdy little boy and how they had been blessed by his coming. Then, when Jamie reached the age of five, they moved to Yellow Creek and three years later, after Ashton's arrival, entered the religious community.

Even under the stringent life of New Caanaland, Jamie had remained their father's favorite. Margaret's resentment grew and she constantly sought ways to belittle Jamie or to place blame on him for things real or imagined. Sometimes she felt she had succeeded in supplanting this invidious competitor for her father's love, only to see Jamie forgiven whatever trespass he'd made and returned to the pedestal on which she imagined her father placing him. Her estrangement from her father caused Margaret to transfer her affection to Bradley Ashton.

During the two years that followed her initiation into the newly created Sisterhood, Ashton continued his practice of roaming the West as an itinerant preacher, selecting converts and sending them along to New Caanaland. As a result, he called on Margaret's favors infrequently. She was forced to satisfy her constantly growing sexual demands through secret, and dangerous, liaisons with some of the gunmen-deacons. She found them unimaginative and unfulfilling. To feed her constant lust, Margaret sought release with others in the Sisterhood who, like herself, found themselves excessively stimulated and lacking outlets. Although she

71

found these interludes pleasant, they fell far short of her expectations.

Margaret's sharp, devious mind quickly realized that the key to love and admiration in her future was the same as the key that unlocked Bradley Ashton's inner being. She determined to learn everything she could about him. Overcoming her repugnance toward her little brother, she sought out Jamie.

She wanted to question her brother regarding the apparent inconsistency of the Reverend Master teaching the boys to loathe and fear the very thing *he* prized the most. After initial suspicion, Jamie proved quite talkative.

"Well . . . you're sure you aren't askin' this just to get me in trouble again? Promise? Sure, then. The Rev'ren' Master told us that was what Sodom and Gomer . . . uh, whatever that other town was called, got punished for. Everybody was bein' nasty and so the Almighty killed 'em all and destroyed their towns. He says it's gonna happen again real soon, too."

That sly devil, Margaret thought of Ashton. That way he saves up the pick of the crop for himself. Right then she set her mind to make herself the blue-ribbon prize of that crop in the Reverend Master's eyes. It took her a year and a half, but now she felt she had become an indispensable part of Ashton's hierarchy. A position from which she could successfully strike back at those who had done her wrong. A place of power and wealth. Then all this had to happen and now she felt suddenly cold as she saw her opportunities slipping through her fingers. With a start, she realized Ashton had started to dismiss the men.

"We'll have the Miller girls back, that's for certain. Larry Don, call a meeting of all deacons for first thing in the morning. We'll ride to Aspen Gap and reclaim our strayed sheep."

Chapter Eight

A light knock at the door disturbed Tanaka Tom Fletcher, who sat at the small table in his room over the Pot O' Gold saloon carefully working fine quality whale oil into the raw steel of his *katana, ho-tachi,* and *tanto*—the two traditional swords and fighting dagger. He put aside his task, keeping the *ho-tachi* in hand, and crossed the room to the door.

"Who is it?"

A soft, feminine voice, muffled by the wooden panel, came in response. "It's Martha . . . Martha Miller."

Tom opened the door and invited her in. He indicated a chair near the table, and once Martha seated herself, asked her indulgence when he returned to his work. They sat in silence for a few moments, Martha wringing a small square of lace-bordered linen handkerchief into a limp scrap before she broke the silence.

"You . . . you probably think me most brazen to come here like this. I mean, to a man's room, me being an unmarried woman."

Tanaka Tom looked up from his oiling and blinked, confused by this. "It would be more moral for a married woman to visit a single man in his room?" He always encountered difficulty understanding the strange customs of this, his native but alien land.

"Oh, no. No. What I meant was . . . well, in polite society it isn't considered proper for a young lady to visit a young gentleman in his room. It would be even worse should one or both of them be married . . . to

73

others than each other, I mean . . . Oooh! I'm making a perfect dither of this. And . . . and you're laughing at me, I can see you are."

In truth, humor glinted from Tanaka Tom's eyes. For all the strangeness of American ways, he found this girl, Martha, to be most attractive. "I am not laughing . . . at least not out loud. That would be impolite, Martha-*san*. In Nippon it is more unforgivable to be impolite than to kill a man. Even if the man is one's enemy, politeness must be maintained. It is a matter of honor."

"You called me 'Martha-*san*.' What does it mean? I heard you speak to the Dorns like that."

"It is a term of politeness. Like saying sir, or lady, madam, or miss. I suppose I should call you Miss Martha, the way others do."

"Yes . . . that is the accepted way. But I like Martha-*san*. I think . . . I prefer it."

"You are kind."

"Those," Martha bobbed her head to indicate the swords. "They are beautiful. Although their purpose is killing and bloodletting, they are really quite beautiful."

Tom felt genuine pleasure at Martha's admiration of his weapons. "Thank you. A samurai's swords are almost sacred things. Each is made by the master armorer only after a long period of reflection. It must express his inward harmony; the time, hour, positions of the planets that circle our globe, all of these things play an important part in his creation in metal. Before going to work on a new blade, he performs an ablution, using pure cold water to keep away evil influences.

"For this ritual he covers his head in black and dresses in clothes of spotless white to symbolize purity. The sword, as it is made, obtains a sort of sacredness from this. It becomes a *being* in its own right, with a personality of its own, having a soul, like man, and therefore we always handle these objects with the greatest respect and reverence." Tom smiled shyly, embarrassed by his sudden loquaciousness.

Seeing the rapt attention on Martha's face, however,

he felt emboldened to continue. "Did you know that each part of the sword, and its scabbard, has a name? Not merely a description of what they are, their function. It's much more than that. The names describe the portion referred to in much the same relationship as the names of the parts of the body. For instance, your liver is not what causes you to live, nor does a kidney make jokes." Despite herself, Martha giggled at Tom's simile. "You see what I mean. There is a living relationship between name and part and the whole.

"Here. This gold pommel cap," Tom hurried on, lifting his *katana* from the table. "It is called a *kashira*, which more nearly means 'seat of power,' than it does the thing that holds the tang inside the handle. See what I'm getting at? And this, the sharkskin wrapping is called *uchi-himo*, the silk cords over that, *mekugi*, yet *uchi-himo* literally means 'inside wrapping' and *mekugi* means 'binding.' Together they make up the *tsuka*, or handle, that includes the pommel. The two decorated faces of the hilt are called *seppa*, together they form the hilt itself, or *tsuba*. This fitted gold piece in front that holds the *tsuba* in place is called *habaki*, the blade itself, *katana*, after its type.

"Now, here," Tom rushed on with boyish enthusiasm, "take the scabbard. It is called a *saya*. This gold end cap is the *kojiri*. These cord wrappings of silk, *sageo*, and the jeweled gold band at the open end, *koiguchi kanagu*. That tang that locks the blade in place is the *kogai*, which is held in place on the *saya* by the *kurikata*." Tanaka Tom flashed a brief smile. "That concludes your first lesson in swordsmanship. Although I don't suppose a young lady of refinement came for that purpose."

"No. Yet, I find myself both fascinated and repelled by it all. What I came for, if again you don't think me too bold, is to ask you to have dinner with me. Will you?"

"Might I suggest, rather, a traveler's lunch? A . . . ah . . ." Tom's English failed him.

"Picnic?" Martha supplied.

"Just so. Would you approve of such an arrangement?"

"Oh, yes. That would be marvelous. I shall take care of everything. You may call for me at twelve noon at Maw Tamblin's. Good day, Tom-*san*."

Delighted, Tom laughed aloud. "And to you, Martha-*san*."

Two indignant citizens of Aspen Gap scurried off the boardwalk into the mud-gummed street to avoid a collision with Travis McNee and Clive Niebocker. The two bounty hunters stomped along, shoulder to shoulder, filling the narrow walk between the building fronts and support posts. McNee's patience had worn thin.

"The devil take these people. To hear them, you'd believe they never seen nothin'. Not heard of a feller named Fletcher, don't recognize the description, don't know about any new fellers in town. Nothin'! Well, don't you believe one word of it. Not for a second. Tom Fletcher is in this town and we're gonna find him."

"We did! We did!" Clive shouted excitedly, arm extended, agitated hand pointed toward the next intersection.

McNee looked up to see an open-top barouche, with a sleekly groomed pair of roan Arabs drawing it, cross the center of Main Street and disappear behind the buildings on Third. Driving the rig, he noticed, was a tall, thin man with dark hair, a whispy, drooping moustache and sun-darkened, olive-brown skin. McNee gawked at the sight, making a mental comparison with the description of the man they sought. Then his tobacco juice-stained lips split wide in a satisfied grin and he clapped an arm around his partner's shoulder.

"We-e-l-l-l, I'll be hanged as a chicken thief. You're right, Clive. By jing, that's him sure as I'm borned."

"Let's go git him, then, huh, Trav?"

"Now don't go gettin' yourself all riled up, Clive. This town's a mite too small to not know every soul in it and what each one has for breakfast. Yet they tell us

76

they never heared of a Tom Fletcher. That means he's some sort of special person to them, right? We don't wanna go off half-cocked. We'd best follow him a while, might be we can catch him alone somewhere and . . . ah, make the capture."

Tanaka Tom Fletcher reined the team to a halt in front of Maw Tamblin's boarding house and climbed down to assist Martha with a huge hamper basket she carried as she came down the front steps. He set the lead pyramid hitching anchor on the ground and fastened its swivel snap in the bridle ring of the wheel horse.

"You're right on time, Tom-*san* . . . ah, Mr. Fletcher."

"Why the sudden formality, Martha-*san*?"

"Ah, well, we . . . we're in public now."

"Your customs are as inconsistent here as they are strange. Will I call you Miss Miller?" He effected a deep, courtly bow that brought a tinkling trill of giggles from Martha Miller.

"Oh, pooh with that, with all of it, Tom-*san*. See what I brought?" She opened the hamper Tom had placed in the space behind the padded leather front seat. Nestled in a large red-checked napkin lay a generous stoneware bowl of fried chicken. Another mound turned out to fresh-baked bread, still warm from the oven, and a lump of sweet butter. Sliced boiled potatoes in a dill and vinegar sauce occupied another bowl and the remaining space was shared by a ripe, mellow cheese, apples, and some grapes.

"It looks delicious, but it's more than any two people can eat. Are others coming along?"

"No, silly. Just the two of us. The ride in this mountain air will enlarge your appetite." Martha re-did the food coverings while Tom retrieved the anchor and put it in its proper place. He helped her aboard and took his own seat, snapping the team into a trot with the reins.

"There's a meadow not far outside town. Maw Tamblin told me about it. We can be alone there . . . to enjoy our meal."

"You'll have to give me directions."

"Turn here, then again onto Main and out of town toward the gap up there east of town."

Fifteen minutes later the scenery had changed drastically. Gone were the streaming, mud-sloppy streets and raw wood buildings of Aspen Gap, replaced by myriad dancing wild flowers, delicately-quaking pale green leaves on white trunked aspen trees and the pervading scent of pine boughs and sap perfumed the air. Birds sang and insects hummed lazily. Tom guided the team off the road and up the hillside toward a towering cottonwood, in the same moment Martha pointed out the meadow. Venerable with age, the hoary old tree spread fat branches to provide a wide pool of shade on the grassy slope at its base. They dismounted and Tom spread a blanket upon which Martha laid out the food.

"I brought a bottle of wine," Martha said brightly as she produced a dusty green container from the basket.

"Too bad it isn't *saki* or *Koketsu* plum wine," Tom commented.

Martha frowned, the shallow wrinkles on her forehead making her even more appealing to look at. "Oh, then this one disappoints you?"

"Not at all, if you selected it. Only that the others are ideal for a meal such as this . . . and they remind me of home. Let's eat. You were right about the mountain air making me hungry."

Travis McNee crouched in a cluster of boulders at the notch of a saddle-back some five hundred yards beyond and above the spot where Tanaka Tom and Martha enjoyed their food. He held a worn pair of artillery fieldglasses to his eyes and examined the scene with careful attention to detail. A grunt of satisfaction escaped him as he lowered the binoculars and crawled slowly over the ridge to rejoin Clive.

"They're there, like we figgered, Clive. All cuddled

up sippin' high-priced wine and gobblin' grub like two starved miners. It'll be easy, nothin' to it."

"What about the girl?"

"We cain't afford to have no witnesses. We'll plug her, too, an' claim he did it."

"All right by me. But . . . cain't we . . . you know, can't we have a little fun first?"

McNee frowned disapprovingly at his partner. "That ain't ethical, Clive. You know that."

Clive looked chastened. "You gonna make the shot, Trav? You're better with a rifle than me."

"That's the way I figgered it. Now let's get goin'."

Silently they crept back into position. McNee brought along a well-cared for .50-caliber Sharps buffalo rifle. When he'd wriggled himself into the position he felt satisfied with, he rested the heavy barrel on a boulder top and took careful aim. Approving of the sight picture and setting, he eared back the big hammer and once more squinted through the buckhorns, lining up the front blade on Tanaka Tom's head. Gently his trigger finger began taking up slack.

Chapter Nine

Tanaka Tom bent forward to select an apple when the fat .50-caliber bullet sizzled through the empty air where his head had been a moment before. It buried itself in the fat Gouda. The weight and velocity of the slug exploded the cheese all over the blanket and both persons. A fraction of a second later, Tom heard the dull thud of the detonated round.

"Down!" he shouted, springing away from the blanket and retrieving his Winchester Henry from the floorboards of the rig. He levered off two fast rounds, hearing them whine and shriek off the distant rocks where a telltale puff of greasy, gray-white smoke revealed the location of the hidden assassin. Again the big Sharps boomed, and wood splintered on one side of the barouche, frightening the team into foot-stamping confusion. Tom fired again and a second gun among the rocks joined the battle. The Six-gun Samurai took more care with his next one, spanging lead off a big boulder at a point he figured would be head-high to one of the killers. He felt pleased as a yelp of pain rewarded his efforts. Then he threw the .44 to his shoulder again.

Sudden movement among the rocks brought a fury of fire from Tanaka Tom's Winchester, until its tubular magazine ran dry. Cursing his bad fortune, he began to reload hurriedly. He looked up, his task only half completed, in time to see two horsemen charging down on them. One held a rifle, the other clutched a revolver, both firing wildly in the general direction of Tom and

Martha. Bullets whined through the air as Tanaka Tom dashed to more substantial cover behind the fat bole of the cottonwood.

Tom took careful aim this time and squeezed off a round. The blunt-nosed, 200-grain slug smashed into the broad chest of Niebocker's charging mount at a velocity of 1,125 feet per second, bursting the valiant animal's heart and spilling horse and rider onto the ground in a dangerous heap of flying arms, legs, and iron-shod hooves. Quickly Tanaka Tom changed to the other target and sent three fast rounds burning down range. Travis McNee wheeled abruptly at the sound of his partner's panicked cry and rode back to him, one arm extended. Ignoring the danger of turning his back on their former target, McNee effected a running mount rescue, Clive swinging his leg over the bobbing rump of Travis's horse. Roundly cursing their ill fate, the two men rode off out of range and, a moment later, out of sight.

Tom rushed to the team, calming them and starting to unhitch one.

"What are you doing?" Martha demanded, her voice tight with fear.

"I'm going after them."

"Oh, no. Please don't. I'd be terrified here alone." She came to Tom, arms out, encircling his neck. "Oh, Tom, Tom. T-they were trying to k-k-kill us. Oh, hold me. Hold me tightly. I'm so afraid."

Her body trembled violently and her knees threatened to give way. Tom put his own arms around her and then lifted her, carrying Martha to the blanket. Tom gently placed her there and started to disengage his arms. Suddenly, they were both on the blanket, clinging to each other.

Martha felt an unexplainable longing, a desire to touch and be touched by this powerful, silent man who had but moments before saved her life. She clung to him despite the security of the ground beneath her back and her eyes spoke eloquently of the unfamiliar need and consuming desire to which she could not put words.

Tanka Tom noted this change amid growing wonderment.

He recognized the nature of the emotions coursing through Martha's body and, to his surprise, discovered a mutual response welling up within himself. With this knowledge came the realization he could not possibly take up pursuit of their would-be assassins. It would be unspeakably cruel to leave Martha in her present excited state, although Tom was aware that in her innocence, Martha no doubt remained entirely unaware of how her body betrayed its innermost desires.

Martha's fear had blinded her to that also, although Tom's worldly cynical side told him that all her clinging wasn't motivated by fear alone. Now, no matter how detached Tom tried to remain, he found himself becoming aroused by the heady aroma of her mounting passion. He bent his face to her and their lips met. Martha's, cold at first, warmed to lively participation and she made no effort to resist when Tanaka Tom cupped one small, pert breast in his hand and pressed gently against the nipple, affirming his impressions when he felt it hardening under his ministrations. Martha broke off their embrace with a mumbled endearment.

Tom caught Martha's dimpled chin between the thumb and forefinger of his left hand and drew her back to him, his lips bruising hers in the intensity of his growing desire. His other hand abandoned its diligent manipulation of her breast and began fumbling with the buttons at the back of her dress. Martha twisted her lips from his and pushed herself away with a small hand against Tom's broad chest.

"No," she begged through panting passion. "Please, not any more. We . . . we've gone . . . too far." Tom ended Martha's protest by covering her mouth with his, tongue seeking entry, while he used his superb strength to draw them into a sitting position.

Both of Tom's hands began working at the buttons of Martha's dress, her feeble struggles contained in his powerful arms, protests muffled by his searching mouth. With an effort he freed Martha's shoulders, pulled her arms from the sleeve holes and drew the cloth down over her vibrant young body, bunched it below her slender waist so that it revealed the ruffled bodice she wore beneath. A small moan escaped from Martha's throat.

Martha found her mind a whirl of confusion, her body trembling with a heretofore unexperienced desire. Part of her cried out at this violation of her person, while the remainder raged with eager expectation of what might come next. To her growing delight, Tom took little time in revealing this to her.

With swift motions, Tom jerked the chemise over her head, exposing her youthfully firm, pink-tipped breasts. Martha felt a shiver of delight as the cool autumn mountain breeze played over her naked flesh, then Tom took her in his arms again, lips crushing hers, tongue probing with a will of its own until she felt a shock of joyful warmth as it entered her mouth. With a thrill she realized Tom had not yet achieved the full extent of his conquest.

Tom's hands began exploring the silken softness of Martha's lovely body, sliding over the sleekness of her ribs, down to the narrow closure of her waist and proud flare of her not-quite womanly hips. With a start he realized he had become more aroused than he could ever recall, his manhood tumescent, the foreskin withdrawn and painfully stretched. He wanted this tender young girl more than any woman he'd ever encountered.

His hands went to the buckle of his gunbelt, loosened it. He fumbled with the buttons of his Levis, opening them. Martha gasped when Tom undid the wrappings of his Japanese style underclothes and the great fullness of him surged into view. In that instant any pretense at conventional defense of her virtue fled from her. She broke away, hurriedly divested herself of the remainder of her clothing and lay back on the blanket, legs spread invitingly, body panting and heaving with desire. Tom seemed to loom over her as she opened her mouth, the words gasping out.

"I . . . I've n-never been with a man before, Tom.

T-this is my first time. Be gentle with me, please. But hurry, my darling sweet Tom, oh, please hurry!"

Without speaking, Tom reached out for her, lifting her from the blanket. Then he lay on his back and guided Martha until she poised atop him, legs astraddle. With Tom's help she lowered herself until his burning flesh met her eager moistness. In the next instant they were joined as he entered her, slowly and deeply.

When they returned to Aspen Gap, Tom steered the rig sharply away from Main Street a block sooner than usual. Late afternoon sun slanted weakly across the mountain valley that contained the small mining town, casting elongated shadows, making the buggy wheels into egg-shaped, flickering objects from a fantasy world. Martha, her eyes still sparkling and slightly unfocused from her gentle, but passionate, entry into womanhood, did not see the cause of the unusual change in direction, her thoughts still fixed on the three glorious times Tom Fletcher had joined his body with hers. She remained unaware of the present until Tanaka Tom pulled to a stop in front of Maw Tamblin's boarding house. The silence continued while Tom dismounted and came around to Martha's side of the carriage, his mind on what he had seen.

The Six-gun Samurai's sharp eyesight had taken in a scene two blocks along Main that caution dictated he avoid. He did so particularly for Martha's sake. A man Tom assumed by his size and build to be Bradley Ashton, dressed now in ordinary clothes (except for the black-and-white dickey of a clergyman) and accompanied by five others, harangued the sheriff in front of the city jail. Tom also decided that as soon as he could reasonably free himself from Martha he wanted a closer look at what was going on.

"Oh, darling Tom, this has been, I mean, the most wonderful day of my . . . my life," Martha breathed in a near-whisper as Tom helped her from the barouche. She leaned against him possessively, craving continued physical contact. Tom took her by both

84

shoulders and gently held her away from him, fingers softly caressing her trembling body.

"Martha. By the standards of your world we mustn't make a . . . ah, scene is it? We must behave with decorum, as though nothing happened. We'll discuss this . . . us . . . at another time. There *will* be other . . . happy times for us, yes?"

"Oh, yes, my dearest, yes. Good-bye for now."

"Good-bye," Tom replied as he escorted Martha to the front door, their picnic hamper in one hand. "I . . . enjoyed the afternoon."

Martha recovered herself enough to affect the proper tone of polite indifference expected by society. "And I, too, Mr. Fletcher. Do call again. Good day."

"And to you, Miss Martha." Tom suppressed a grin of near-boyish delight at this charade while he hurried to the rig and headed toward Main Street.

"They have broken the law, Sheriff. As a peace officer, you can understand that, surely?" Having tried demands and bluster, Ashton now sought another tack.

"What laws have they broken?" Harvey Wellman's voice held a cold, stubborn edge. In the background Tanaka Tom reined in the team to listen carefully to the argument.

"Why, the laws of New Caanaland, the laws of the church and . . . and the Almighty's laws. They are more than runaway girls, as I first told you, they are criminals and you are duty bound to turn them over to us for proper trial and punishment."

"Precisely what sort of punishment did you have in mind, *Mister* Ashton? A nice little flogging with a cat-o'-nine-tails? Or locking them up to starve and roast in a tiny little tin box out in the blazing sun? We know all about your means of punishment and, whether you are aware of it or not, they are not countenanced under the laws of the United States. You have no jurisdiction here, and there are no warrants outstanding on the Miller girls in this part of the Territory. Therefore I am under no obligation to surrender them to you, and I haven't the least damn intention of doing so. Pack up your rabble and get out of this town, *Mister* Ashton."

"His proper title is the Reverend Master, Sheriff. You'd be wise to use it." A light of fury and a certain madness flared in Margaret Dorn's closely set eyes. "This is a matter of religion, something you seem to ignore. Your secular laws and procedures have no precedence here. It is the Almighty's will we must obey. *Give us those girls!*"

"Religion is it?" Sheriff Wellman drawled sarcastically to Margaret, then turned his attention to Bradley Ashton. "You know what you can do with your godless travesty of a religion, don't you? You can take it and shove it up your ass, *Mister* Ashton!"

Ashton paled and rocked back on his heels as though he had been struck. "Anathema!" he cried. "You shall all be struck down, as were Sodom and Gomorrah. Blasphemers, defilers of the temple, children of Satan! All of you in this town, take warning. Your days are numbered! Surely as the sun sinks in the sky each night, your lives shall be snuffed out and your town become a barren waste in the wilderness. Beware the wrath of the Almighty! Beware the wrath of the anointed of New Caanaland!"

Suddenly Ashton whirled away, swinging into the saddle of his gray gelding. "Come, let us seek an answer in prayer. We shall return with fire and sword to do the Lord's work."

When the three gunslingers, the stolid farmer, Margaret Dorn, and Ashton galloped off into the dusty distance, Sheriff Harvey Weller shook his head in disgust. "Crazy people. Every last one of them, stark raving crazy."

"I wouldn't count those three gunslicks among the lunatics, Sheriff," Tanaka Tom advised from the seat of the buggy. "I think it is well overdue that something be done about Ashton and his flock."

Chapter Ten

Early the next morning, Tanaka Tom prepared to leave Aspen Gap for New Caanaland. He did not take his magnificent Morgan stallion, nor did he dress in his usual way.

Loose-legged gray cotton trousers covered Tom's powerfully muscled legs, a plain brown flannel shirt over his broad chest; he wore no footwear of any sort. He left behind his Colt .44 and Winchester Henry carbine, concealing only his *ho-tachi* and *tanto* in the sparse packs on his mule. Martha Miller found him at the livery stable.

"Where are you going in that outlandish get-up?" she demanded lightly, her deep, vernal love glowing from her face.

"To Yellow Creek. Something must be done to stop Ashton. He grows more insane . . . and dangerous every day."

Fearful understanding caused Martha's voice to falter. "Y-you're . . . going to . . . kill him . . . aren't you?"

"Yes. Eventually. But for reasons of my own. If, in the process, I do good for others . . . for you . . . it is your *karma*, as well as mine. Do you understand?"

Martha frowned, uncertain of his meaning. Then anxiety crumpled her face. "Don't go. Please don't go. He's as clever as the Devil himself and he'll suspect you, he'll find out and have you killed. Oh, Tom, I couldn't stand it if I lost you now. After all, darling, now that we're . . . we're engaged."

A look of surprise crossed Tanaka Tom's face. He felt a genuine puzzlement. "Engaged? What does that mean . . . this engaged?"

Martha's blue eyes opened widely. "Why, to get married. After . . . after . . ." she leaned close and lowered her voice so that the crotchety old man that ran the livery would not hear. "Well, we were . . . intimate together, weren't we? And . . . when that happens . . . it means we are in love and are engaged to be married."

Tom kept his face impassive, but his mind whirled with consternation. Of all the strange customs of his native land, this one—of which he'd just heard—had to be the oddest. He had been brought up in Japan to look on sex as a necessary and healthy outlet for both men and women, something good for one's peace of mind and body. What did that have to do with marriage? Marriages were arranged by the elders of one's family and rarely were the partners consulted as to choice. On the other hand, sex for pleasure, or the release of tensions as had been the case for them, was merely a more satisfactory and grown-up form of *senzuri o kakimas'*, a practice of children. Before Tom could frame a reply, Martha rushed on.

"Oh, please don't go. I love you so. Now that I have you, I don't want to lose you."

"We all lose those we love sooner or later. Let me explain.

"Ashton was one of a band of men who murdered my American family a long time ago. Now it is his turn to die for it. If I die also, that, too, is *karma*."

"You're the one who doesn't understand. He has all those gunmen out there, big, mean men. They . . . they'll have no mercy."

Tanaka Tom smiled tolerantly. "A samurai makes many poems, called *haiku*, in his days to celebrate the gentleness in his life. But it is not that for which he is

88

best known. *Bushido,* the way of the warrior, is the harshest of all masters. You will be here when I return?"

"Yes. Oh, yes, my darling. But . . ."

Without waiting for the rest of Martha's reply, Tom swung onto the mule and, using a willow switch, prodded it into a trot, heading west out of Aspen Gap.

Behind him, Martha stood alone in the dusty street outside the livery. One hand strayed to her throat as though to stifle a sob, the other raised in tearful farewell.

By pushing hard, Tanaka Tom arrived in the valley of Yellow Creek a short while before darkness fell. The last several miles he had covered on foot. He had sifted dust onto his hair and clothes and led his tired mule, so that he looked the part of a penitent who sought salvation. He feigned surprise and fear when, as he expected, two of Ashton's gunslingers braced him on the trail and demanded to know his reason for being there.

"I am Thomas," he answered them in a humble and contrite voice, eyes on the ground. "I come seeking forgiveness and salvation. It is said in the mining camps that Reverend Ashton has made a paradise on earth in this valley. Is this true?"

Ignoring Tom's question, one gunslick spoke to the other. "What you think, Jake?"

Jake Skagen ran one hand over his bristle-stubbled cheeks, which bulged with a cut of tobacco, pursed his thick, brown-stained lips—heightening for Tom the illusion of the south end of a north-bound cow—and squirted out a long, tawny stream of juice that splattered in the dust at Tanaka Tom's feet. "He shore ain't armed, that's fer certain sure, Loren."

Tanaka Tom gave them a benign smile that masked his true feelings about their ignorance. The staff with which he plied the rutted path was in fact a *Bo* stave, or *rokushakubo,* a six foot long, specially hardened oak shaft used in the art of *bojutsu,* a weapon more deadly than a combined club and spear to one wise in its ways.

Choking back the contempt he felt for these slovenly, ill-trained gunmen, Tom tried to make his voice even more humble.

"Well, sir, did I find the right place?"

Loren Greun, heavy-set and the elder of the two, answered him sarcastically. "I suppose you didn't see the sign back there a ways?"

"Oh, yes, sir. Only I can't read," Tom lied easily.

Loren grunted. "You found the place all right. Now we gotta take you in an' see if the Reverend Master will let you stay. Do you have any money?"

"I have forsaken the search for gold and taken a vow of poverty."

"Huh! Might not go so good for you, what with nothin' to he'p fill the coffers. The Rev'ren' Master's mighty partial about that. Howsomever, let's get to goin'."

"Please, sir. I-I am a man of peace. I have turned my face from violence. Your guns disturb me. Does everyone here go about armed?"

Jake Skagen snorted derisively. "Nope. Just us, uh, deacons. We sort of guard the place."

"Then Thomas is in your brave protection, good sirs. Please, take me to the, uh, Reverend Master."

"Right you are, Holy Joe," Skagen sneered, swooping low from his saddle to link arms with Tanaka Tom.

The Six-gun Samurai fought every instinct of his nature to prevent him from smashing the skull of someone so stupid and rude as to defile a person of his class in such a way. His *ki*, that internal, mental force behind the physical powers of his martial arts skills, held him rooted to the ground as though planted in the earth. The result of this sent Jake Skagen sprawling in the dust and pebbles of the rudimentary trail. Vile and colorful curses roared from Skagen's throat as he scrambled to his feet. One of Jake's hands brushed at the dirt clinging to his lips while the other flashed toward his six-gun.

"Oh, no. Please, no!" Tom pleaded, gritting his teeth to remain obsequious in the face of his true nature. He extended both arms, hands turned palm outward in a gesture of avoidance and peace. "I . . . I meant no harm. Perhaps I am heavier than I appear. An accident, nothing more, yes, sir?"

"You damn fool Bible-thumper. You almost got me a busted tooth. I oughtta . . ."

"Take it easy, Jake," Loren commanded. "Maybe he's right. Anyhow, we gotta take him to Ashton, right?"

"Thank you, thank you for my life," Tom babbled, shuffling side-ways toward Skagen's horse. "You wish me to mount, yes? Then we can ride in like friends."

"Damn Chink." Growling in suppressed fury, Skagen mounted and Tom swung up behind him, keeping well back of the saddle, one hand clutching the mule's lead rope. The image of the cringing, cowering creature his role demanded made the Six-gun Samurai want to vomit, but he reminded himself that he needed an inside look at Ashton's community before he could make intelligent plans. The only ones who got in were the righteous, so he must playact the appearance of such a one at his craven worst. Without another word, Loren led them out toward the distant buildings.

"Well, what do we have here?" Bradley Ashton asked as he strutted out onto the porch of his parsonage. He wore a white robe, the cowl thrown back, and wiped at his greasy fingers daintily with a lace-bordered linen napkin. He resented the interruption of his dinner, but the sight of this unwelcome visitor intrigued him.

"We caught him out on the cast road, Rev'ren'," Loren Greun explained. "Says he wants to join the community."

"What's your name, fellow?" Ashton snapped.

"I am called Thomas." Tanaka Tom let his gaze drop to the ground. "I seek a life of contemplation and penance for my sins."

"You've come to the right place for that. Tell me, Brother Thomas, have you renounced the evils of capitalism and the bourgeois society outside this valley?"

"Yes, Reverend Master."

"Are you willing to surrender to the Brotherhood all that you possess so that it may be put to the use and benefit of everyone equally?"

"All that I own I have with me and I have taken a vow . . ."

"He ain't got no money, Rev'ren' Master," Skagen's voice cut out Tom's.

"Hummm. Well then, are you willing to labor in the vineyards of the Lord?"

"Yes, Reverend Master. That and any other task you put me to."

"Well spoken. Well spoken indeed." Ashton's face beamed with a sudden smile. He liked the looks of this one. His eyes dwelt long on Tom's broad shoulders, stature and the obvious strength of the legs that held the man upright. He might be all the humble and contrite fellow now, but in a fight, Ashton estimated, he could prove most formidable. When it came to a showdown with the people of Aspen Gap over the Miller girls, it would do well to have one like this on his side, the tainted reverend decided. He raised his hand in benediction.

"It is decided then. You shall stay here in New Caanaland, Brother Thomas, and spend your days in prayer and meditation, laboring for the common good. I must warn you. As a candidate for membership in our Holy Brotherhood, you must be diligent in your efforts to prove yourself worthy. You shall constantly be tested to show you are developing a proper frame of mind and molding the discipline to control the desires of your physical being. When the Spirit of the Lord visits you and you are truly born again, we shall welcome you into our sacred community."

Travis McNee bought another whisky for the barfly who hung slack-kneed from the far end of the pine-plank counter in the Trail's End saloon on a side street in Aspen Gap. The old rum-dumb had babbled freely enough about knowing the whereabouts of the Miller girls until McNee bought the first round. Then he became close-mouthed, letting a few words be pried out with each renewed jigger of rot-gut. With this filling of his shotglass, his monologue dried up entirely.

"Now dang it, Jethro, you said you knew those females I was lookin' to meet an' where they hung out, ain't that the truth?"

"S-sure, sure it is, Trav, m'friend. Right as rain. An' it ain't far from here, nuther. Just g-go up a, uh, urrrph," Jethro paused to belch a miasma of sour whisky fumes and lick his lips. "Just go on up a block from here an' turn to yer left. Then take another block an' you ain't very far away then. Uh . . . say, uh, all this here talkin' sure makes a feller dry," he wheedled, then lifted his glass and downed the contents. He pushed it toward the far side of the bar with dirty, crack-nailed fingers, while he turned a beggar's face toward McNee.

Trav McNee lost all semblance of patience. The bounty hunter reached out, grabbed the shabby lapels of Jethro's grimy coat and slammed the old drunk violently against the wall. "Listen to me, you soggy-brained old sot. You're gonna wind up suckin' on the muzzle of my forty-four instead of a whisky bottle iffin you don't answer my goddamned questions. Talk, damnit!" McNee's words lashed at Jethro's blotched, broken-veined face.

The old boozer's eyes went wide and color slowly drained from his whisky-red nose, while tears pooled up and overflowed to make light-hued streaks down his bristly cheeks. His mouth gaped and worked spasmodically, trying to form words.

"All right, all right, all right!" he managed at last. "Please don't hurt me, Mr. McNee. Please. They's stayin' at Maw Tamblin's. That's over on Murdock. Like I said, it's up a block and over one, then two on Murdock. Big ol' place in the middle of the block. They says that the big guy with the swords is sweet on the older Miller girl. You find them girls an' you'll find him, too."

Trav McNee shoved the drunken Jethro away from

him and turned on one heel. He stalked to a table where Clive Niebocker sat playing cards and idly asking questions about Fletcher. "Okay. We got what we wanted."

Clive folded his hand and followed Travis McNee out the door. Once away from curious ears, he tugged at McNee's shirt sleeve. "Ya mean we found Fletcher?"

"No. But we have a line on him. I say we have a little chat with these two Miller girls and wring out of them exactly where our boy Tom Fletcher happens to be."

Chapter Eleven

"Why are you doing this? What do you want with me?" Martha Miller demanded angrily when Travis McNee removed the gag from her mouth. She looked around the dimly lightened room, her eyes taking in the dreary, abandoned atmosphere. There was a pile of dusty, broken furniture shoved into a corner, next to it the cracked, rotting leather straps of a long-unused bunk, here, beside the chair in which she sat, was a rickety table, empty except for a battered kerosene lamp, its wick turned low to emit the only light in the tumbledown shack on the edge of Aspen Gap. Once more she voiced her demands.

"Why did you bring me here? What do you want?"

"We got a few questions we want you to answer, sweetie." Clive Niebocker's face, seemingly disembodied, bobbed before her in the yellow light like a gibbous moon.

Martha tried to muster control of her trembling body behind a haughty demeanor. "Whatever could I possibly know that would interest the likes of you?"

A meaty palm smacked against one cheek, wrenching Martha's head to the side and unbidden tears of pain ran from her eyes. "Don't get uppity with us, cousin," Travis McNee growled from the darkness on her right. "We know you saw a lot of a certain man we're interested in. Where is he now?"

Tom Fletcher! Now that the mystery had been taken

out of it, Martha tightened her resolve, vowing to say nothing. "I don't know what you're talking about."

"You damn well know him good enough to go on a picnic with him!" Clive shouted, poking his face close to hers.

"Y-you're the ones that took shots at us?"

"Not at you, Missy, at him. He's a wanted man, a criminal and we're tracking him down. Now talk."

Martha turned her head to look into the gloom at the speaker. Travis McNee grinned wickedly, exposing two missing teeth. When he observed her involuntary shudder, he continued to press his advantage.

"Harboring a criminal is a crime in itself. You'd best be for helpin' us, Missy. Women's Prison does awful things to a girl's looks."

"I don't know anything to help. And I don't believe you. Tom would never do . . ." Martha stopped abruptly, sinkingly aware that she had betrayed her own promise to keep silent.

"So, he's Tom to you, is he?" McNee seized his advantage with the instinct of a professional hunter. "Say now, I bet he got in your pantaloons, eh? Hoisted your skirts right proper did he?" Martha blushed furiously while the two bounty hunters exchanged knowing glances and laughed lewdly. McNee's big hand flashed out again, slapping Martha soundly.

"You don't expect us to believe that someone beds a pretty little thing like you then up and pulls stakes, do you? *Where did he go?*"

Martha recoiled from the demanding voice as best her bonds would allow. "I-I don't know. H-He just . . . rode out. To Denver, maybe," she lied ineffectually.

Travis McNee slapped Martha again and an instant later Clive Niebocker grabbed her by both shoulders, shaking her violently. "No more lies, ya hear? We can do this the easy way or the hard one. That's up to you. Either way, you *will* talk."

Martha's eyes darted frantically around the room, avoiding contact with her tormentors, as she struggled to make up more lies, think of anything to stall and misdirect them. Niebocker closed in again, menacing, hulking. Martha squeezed her eyes tightly shut.

"H-how can I tell you something I do not know? If I did, I wouldn't anyway."

McNee grunted. "We'll see about that."

Martha felt the menacing presence of the two men close in on her. Niebocker reached out with one grubby hand and ripped downward from the neck of her dress, tearing the cloth away from her shoulder and exposing one pink breast. With a calloused finger and thumb he pinched the nipple, a horny, dirty nail biting deeply into flesh. Marth's face crumpled with pain and she writhed with agony and revulsion, yet she managed to choke back the scream that rose in her throat. Then she felt a loosening of the rope that bound her body to the chairback.

The two bounty men abruptly lifted Martha, her hands and feet still securely tied, and dumped her onto the table. Clive Niebocker stepped backward out of her sight and quickly undid the rope binding her legs. He reached out and roughly pulled up her skirt and petticoats, then began tugging at her underclothes. Martha gasped in shock.

"You filthy swine!" she cried, her body writhing.

Travis McNee leaned down by her ear, his voice a wicked whisper. "Maybe we oughta git a little of what that Fletcher feller got from you. After two or three times each, you might get to likin' it."

"Y-you wouldn't dare," Martha shot back. "You'd be nothing better than animals, beasts."

"Whatever you say, Missy. All the same, we'd be havin' our fun while we was at it. Now, *answer my questions*!"

"No! No! I don't know anything, please leave me alone."

"Last chance, Missy, before I let Clive have you."

Clive had completed his task, the bunched cloth of Martha's underclothes strung tightly between her widespread ankles. Martha trembled with terror, her naked flesh slick with the oily sweat of fear. Her eyes rolled in her head and she frantically tried to will herself not to believe this was happening to her. Clive stepped over the insubstantial barrier, one hand stroking Martha's bare thigh, the other caressing the swelling in the front of his trousers. Then he reached out with both arms, grasped Martha by the bare legs and drew her to the edge of the table. Grinning in abandoned lust, he undid his fly and exposed the stunted uglyness of his small, but engorged manhood.

Martha's face went waxen and her eyes rolled up in her head, tears streaming down her cheeks as she sobbed hysterically. "Oh, no! Please, God, no! Don't do it. I . . . I . . . Oh, no! H-h-he . . . he went to . . . to . . . New Caanaland." Martha's head slumped to one side and her words came out a mumbled, hopeless plea. "Oh, Tom, forgive me. Please forgive me."

"Now, let's hear it all again. Why did he go to that religious phony's place and where will he go from there?" McNee purred close to Martha's ear. He nodded to Clive, who pressed forward, his erect flesh driven against the unwilling body of his victim. Martha looked up, afraid to move now, her eyes glazed her horror, and her words came out mechanically, flat and broken things.

"You are to work here in these fields with the Sisters, Brother Thomas," the guard instructed Tanaka Tom. "You will glean the weeds from around the plants and pick the ripest buds. They are a pale green, but those ready for harvest will take on a slight yellow color and the lips of the buttons will be brownish. When the sacks are filled with ripened fruit, it will be your task to bring them to the vestibule of the church."

The early morning sun had barely risen above the jagged peaks east of New Caanaland and a damp chill hung over the valley. Tom felt that somehow he was on the verge of discovering something elemental, an important clue to the reason behind the blank-faced, dull-eyed, mechanical-man behavior of the people in the village. Peyote buds in the church? His ignorance of Western religions prevented him from automatically making the obvious connection. He'd have to work it out another way. Under a vow of silence, given as penance, for two weeks, Tanaka Tom nodded his understanding and acceptance of the orders. The guard left and the harvest crew set to work.

By mid-afternoon, Tom's clothes had become drenched in sweat and clung stickily to his body. Their noon meal—a bowl of cornmeal mush, half of a raw vegetable somewhat like a turnip, and coarse, grayish bread, washed down by a dipper of clear, cold water from the creek—had been long ago forgotten. None of the girls spoke or hummed although they weren't under a vow similiar to Tom's. Their bovine acceptance of this ceaseless, boring drudgery continued to pique his curiosity. When the sun sailed far past its zenith, the afternoon more than halfway done, the bags of peyote buds were ready to be taken to the church. Tom shouldered all twelve of them, tied by thongs to his staff, which he placed against the back of his neck, Oriental style, his arms looped over the shaft to balance the burden. Without a word or backward glance he trudged up the dusty path to the village square and the church.

Inside the dark, cool buildings, Tom felt relief from the blazing sun. He placed the sacks of peyote buds in the indicated place and prepared to leave. Glancing down the aisle to the altar, memory suddenly supplied the missing piece in his puzzle of conjecture. From his childhood he brought forth images of the small Episcopal church a few miles from the Fletcher plantation and of Sunday services there. In particular he recalled the occasion made of his first Holy Communion. That had to be it!

Ashton was using the peyote for the Communion Host. It accounted for the docile, mindlessness of the people at New Caanaland. Loaded up with enough peyote, they would be susceptible to any suggestion made by the man controlling them. Living in a dream-world existence, unable to distinguish hallucination from reality, they would be as tractable as cattle. What an army of cannon fodder such people would make! They could be led fearlessly into battle, confident that the enemy's weapons could not harm them and die not knowing why or how, overwhelming their enemy by sheer force of numbers. Another thought suddenly chilled him.

Perhaps Ashton's operation did fit in with Edward Hollister's plans. The mad colonel could indeed use a army of such single-minded purpose. He would have to learn more about that aspect. With a shudder of repugnance, Tom quickly left the evil "house of worship."

Tom delayed his return to the field. From the nearby parsonage voices reached his ear through a half-open window. He moved that way with careful stealth. He easily identified the speaker as Ashton.

"We're gonna show that smart-ass sheriff, right, boys? I'll see he's fixed once and for all. Larry Don, Jake, Loren, we're gonna fix 'em all. By sunrise Sunday there won't even be a Aspen Gap.

"We'll get these fine folk here all filled up with peyote, fire 'em up to a killin' mood and then take our army into Aspen Gap. We'll kill everyone there and burn that place to the ground."

Chapter Twelve

Saturday morning, the Sabbath for Ashton's twisted little "Paradise," dawned in a partial overcast, the air even cooler than the day before, giving a hint of coming winter. Early, well before the breakfast bell rang, a wagonload of people from outside the valley arrived. Dour looking and silent, their faces wearing perpetual frowns of disapproval, they rolled to a stop before the parsonage. Brad Ashton personally greeted them.

"Brother Channing, Sister Channing. Welcome to you all."

"We've come to enter this holy communtiy, Brother Ashton." Ashton winced at this unaccustomed familiarity from one of his new converts.

"Caleb, please. His proper title is Reverend Master," the man's wife corrected. "We're so pleased to at last be a part of this great work, Reverend Master."

"And welcome you are. You and your dear children," Ashton amended, his eye taking in the slender, boyish form of a Channing daughter of about eleven years of age. She showed promise. It wouldn't be long and he'd have her in the Sacred Sisters. Bradley Ashton smiled a broad, insincere smile. "You brought along with you the . . . ah . . ."

"Yep. We brung the money from our farm, all in gold like you asked. You ask me, though, and I'd say a bank's the best place fer it."

"Brother Caleb," Ashton chided lightly. "That's precisely where it shall be placed. We have our own bank,

101

right here in New Caanaland. From its resources, all share equally. Each according to his ability, each according to his needs. Here we are one." A frown crossed Ashton's forehead. "Where's the Altman family? Didn't they ride out with you?"

Purity Channing looked embarrassed, a pained expression crossing her apple-cheeked face. Her husband answered for her.

"They ain't coming. They was listenin' to those awful things the Miller girls were sayin' about this place. They up and pulled stakes. Said they wanted to get as far away from this part of the country as they could."

Bradley Ashton flushed dark red with anger. He'd lost a good five thousand dollars now because of those girls. "Blasphemers, that's what those wicked girls are. Lying heretics. They'll burn in Hell-fire for this . . ." he got a firm grip on his murderous emotions and continued quietly. "At least, my dear Brother and Sister, you and your, ah, delightful family are here. Soon the bell will ring to break our fast. Won't you join us?"

"Much obliged."

As though by Ashton's command, the breakfast bell clanged from the communal mess-hall for unmarried persons. Tanaka Tom Fletcher had been standing nearby in order to eavesdrop on the conversation between Ashton and the Channings. Now he headed, along with a growing stream of persons, toward the food. To his skilled observer's eyes, the people appeared more animated than previously, moving about with a certain briskness and anticipation. Tom's awareness of the cause only served to increase his anger toward the evil prophet.

From Ashton's explanation of the rules of the communal society, Tom learned that "communion" was taken twice a week, on the Sabbath and at Wednesday night prayer meeting. Each member of the community, man, woman, and child, was to also take a single "Sacred Cake," as Ashton had called them, every evening during vesper services in the home. The cumulative effect of the powerful drug, Tom speculated, would be wearing thin by the eve of each public ceremonial day. The result would account for the increased vivaciousness he observed among Ashton's flock. His mind mulled over how best he might use this information while he walked toward the steps to the dining hall.

"Glorious day for the Lord, isn't it, Brother?" a florid-faced, big-handed farmer greeted Tanaka Tom as he fell into stride beside him. Tom nodded agreement. The farmer looked contrite.

"Oh, sorry. That's right, you're the new one, ain't ye? Still under the vow of silence." Again Tom agreed with a nod. "Well, all the same, it's a glorious day. I love the first bit of nippy fall air, don't you?"

Tom Fletcher frowned slightly, looked up to the sky and gestured toward the sun as though to say he preferred the warmth of summer. Genially misinterpreting the meaning, the farmer rattled on, his tongue released momentarily from its drug-dulled normal state.

"Praise the Lord indeed, Brother. Soon the fields will be covered with snow and we will have time to repair harnesses and equipment and sing His praises throughout all our days. Hallelujah!" He continued on a silence until they climbed the steps to the dining hall, with Tanaka Tom thinking he'd heard a false note of insincerity in the man's voice. At the top of the risers, the farmer reached out suddenly and touched Tom lightly on one arm, arresting his progress.

"See me when your penance is done. I could use a strong hand to help with my fields. The name's Miller . . . Pete Miller. I suppose you wonder why a bachelor would have a piece of ground all his own. Well, I had a family once. My son and two daughters ran away from here . . . fell into evil ways, they did," Miller went on, his voice raised for the benefit of three overalled men approaching them. When the trio passed beyond into the warm eating hall, he continued in a quieter voice.

"Yep, my youngins is gone off and my woman left me because I let 'em do it. Lord, how I miss 'em." Tanaka Tom, struck by sudden inspiration, silently mouthed the names, "Martha . . . Rachel . . . Davey." Pete Miller's eyes widened in surprise. How could a stranger know their names? He choked back a startled response and ended the conversation in a hopeful near-whisper.

"Yes, I see we do need to talk later on. There's things I can tell you about this place you might not believe, maybe not even want to hear. But I'm determined to say my say and get the truth out. If you've seen my kids and know . . . about this place, nod." At Tom's slight vertical movement of his head, Pete Miller sighed heavily and turned abruptly to the door. He shouldered his way through, his step faltering a moment when he heard a ghostly murmur of voice from behind him.

"I'll remember you, Miller-*san*, if ever I need help."

"O-oh, come, come, come, come. Come to the church in the wildwood, come to the church in the vale." The entire congregation sang the old hymn lustily. The bass voices of several farmers boomed steadily as the worshipers tried, without success, to achieve four-part harmony.

Bradley Ashton, dressed in a golden robe, its cowl thrown back, stood in the pulpit. Behind him at the altar, two deacons were busily heaping peyote buds onto ornate silver platters. When the song ended, Ashton raised both arms, his face glowing with rapture.

"Brothers . . . Sisters . . . it is time to share in the feast of the Lord. Come all ye who are heavy-laden and I shall give you peace. Behold the Lamb of God, Him who taketh away the sins of the world!" From the lectern in front of him Ashton took a peyote button, raised it high for the congregation to see. "When the feast was ended, the Lord took bread, blessed it and distributed it to His disciples, saying, 'This is my body. Take and eat of it that you might see visions of Paradise.'"

Standing near the back of the room, Tanaka Tom felt a stirring of revulsion and slow-burning anger. Little versed in Western theology though he was, he recognized that Ashton's twisted mind had made a sorry jumble out of the rituals of several creeds, all for the purpose of introducing the dream cactus to his congregation as a means of keeping them docile and pliant. A samurai learned respect for the purity of form in all things, particularly in the offices and tenets of his chosen religion, with the same exactitide he applied to sword, bow, and horse. Ashton's perversion of faith made him less than a man, less even than human in the eyes of the Six-gun Samurai. When his own turn came, Tanaka Tom faked taking the peyote. With the deftness of an Oriental magician, he palmed the three buds he was instructed to eat.

After three and a half hours of singing, praying, sermonizing and peyote-munching, the services ended at noon. They would begin again at two that afternoon. Tanaka Tom recalled the quantity of dream cactus consumed; so far, six buds for the adults, four for children. If the same quantities held true for the coming session, all the residents of New Caanaland would be seeing visions springing from their own distorted minds or called forth by the flawed imagery of Bradley Ashton. His mind filled with turmoil, Tom walked toward the dining hall, where a light meal was being prepared.

He could do nothing under the present conditions. Ashton's men had all the guns, the people were already so stupefied by drugs as to be helpless—With the possible exception of Pete Miller. Tom noted when he saw the man, his eyes glowed with hate and determination. The angry farmer had apparently also faked eating the peyote. Yet the two of them stood no chance at all against nearly twenty armed gunmen. Certainly they would never be obliging enough to close in on him where his *bo* staff and *ho-tachi* could easily decimate their ranks. No, his attack, when he made it, would have to come from outside. Deciding that brought him to another point.

What about the raid Ashton spoke of against Aspen Gap? When did the insane preacher intend to ride out of this valley? Tom sought answers to these questions by veering from his original path and heading for the parsonage.

This time he did not have the advantage of an open window. In order to hear what was being said, Tanaka Tom had to work his way to the rear of the house and onto the back porch. Treading carefully to avoid any creaking boards, he worked his way to the exhaust pipe of an unused heating stove located in the room he reasoned to be Ashton's office. Pressing an ear to it, the words from inside came to him clearly.

"What about the bank, Rev'ren'? And the other businesses in town? Are we just gonna burn them down?"

"If you're referring to the money, Larry Don, the answer is no. Cash is nonpartisan, anonymous. No matter how evil people might be, one man's gold spends as cleanly as anyone else's. The riches of Aspen Gap will go a long ways toward achieving my goal. When this religious community folds up, as it eventually must, I will divide the spoils among all of those remaining loyal to me to the end. It is my hope that those funds will make us all enormously rich."

"You mean that's all you're in this for? For money?"

"Can you think of a more noble ambition, Jake?"

Jake Skagen made no reply and the rattle of Ashton's chair as he rose and walked around his desk came tinnily to Tanaka Tom's ear. "Now, to the raid itself. We will feed the people a great deal more peyote this afternoon. Then, toward evening I'll stir them into a religious frenzy and we can ride out for Aspen Gap. I want to be in positon to attack at dawn. One more thing. That new man, Brother Thomas. Bring him to me now, will you please?"

Tanaka Tom barely managed to get away from his listening place and clear of the parsonage before Larry Don came seeking him. The gunslinger located Tom outside the dining hall.

"Th' boss . . . er, the Rev'ren' Master wants to see you. Come with me."

106

Apprehension, anxiety, and uncertainty were as alien to a samurai's nature as kindness, mercy, and vegetarianism are to a savage cannibal. Rather than worry over whether or not he had been exposed as a phony, Tanaka Tom spent the few short seconds it took to cross the bare earth of the village square planning how he could use this to his advantage. Perhaps kill Larry Don and Ashton and make good his escape? The idea was appealing. Lop off the head of the church's leader, and the whole demented paradise would fall apart in no time. When he got to the parsonage, his plans disintergrated into useless dreaming.

More than a dozen men crowded the living room of Ashton's house. Several had their six-guns out, cleaning and oiling them, all of them were heavily armed. It wasn't a part of Tom's plan of revenge to die eliminating one of those responsible, leaving the others without punishment. Prudence demanded that he delay his retribution until he could make his attack from outside, using the element of surprise to full advantage.

"I've had my eye on you, Brother Thomas," Ashton began. "You are a hard and willing worker and your zeal is unsurpassed. I have a special task for you, which, if successful, will lift your penance of silence at once. In order to be successful, though, your faith will undergo a monumental test. Tonight a select group is to be formed and sent as an instrument of the Almighty's vengeance against the heretics of Aspen Gap. I want you to ride at the head of those men. It is to you that the honor falls to draw the first blood for the greater glory of the Lord. You shall be my strong right arm and shall slay the unrighteous and bring low the mighty."

The Six-gun Samurai managed to remain hidden until after the peyote-munching session began again at two. Then he hurried to the stable, saddled his mule and led the creature across a tree-bordered field, toward the distant hills, separating New Caanaland from the road to Aspen Gap. He had to get there in time to warn the people. Once he'd accomplished that, he could get on with his revenge against Ashton. When he made his way clear of the village and scattered lookouts, Tanaka Tom swung into the saddle and drummed his heels into the gray-black mule's ribs.

Tanaka Tom rode for a little over half an hour without pausing, aiming for the ridge and across it to where he could catch the Aspen Gap road. He made it to the top and paused only a few seconds to look back, confirming no pursuit. Then, as he drove the mule to an awkward gallop, a rope snaked out of the rocks and settled its loop around his shoulders and arms. The slip-knot noose jerked right and snatched Tom from his mount.

Chapter Thirteen

To Tom it seemed as though the mule leaped out from beneath him. He felt a mild pain and restriction of movement in both arms and he fell to the ground with a solid smack. More coils whipped out along the length of the rope, seeking to entangle him, yet with deft movements of his imprisoned body, Tanaka Tom evaded them one at a time. He felt a tugging at the lariat and knew that the other end was being dallied around a saddlehorn. A slight dragging and constant tautness told him the horse had been left to keep him pinioned like a calf at branding time. Then he heard a crackling in the underbrush, rapidly drawing near.

Travis McNee came at Tom in a rush, heavy boots kicking and stomping, fists flailing. Clive Niebocker took the other side, swinging a lead-weighted oak stick, a San Francisco policeman's billy club. Despite these nearly impossible odds, Tanaka Tom managed to get first to his knees, then to his feet. If he could only run in the direction of the rope tie-down, he could free himself, he thought. Tom's plan collapsed a moment later, like his body, when Clive cracked him painfully across the back of his calves with the weighted baton. McNee immediately began kicking at Tom's head and chest.

Arms held fast to his sides, Tom could not avoid all of the blows. His ears rang and the pain became a constant raw savaging inside him. He fought to keep his eyes focused, lost that battle, too, and moaned softly as darkness enfolded him.

"Christ! I'd hate like hell fightin' him when he weren't tied," Clive gusted out. He spat on the ground beside Tom's head.

"Let's sling him over that mule and get out of here," Travis McNee ordered.

"Why not finish him off here an' now, then head in for our reward?"

"He's gotta be gunshot or some law-dog might ask us a lot of embarrassin' questions. Them Holy Joes down in the valley there might be crazy as a moonstruck coyote, but those gunslingers workin' for 'em'll come swarmin' up here like bats outta hell iffin we shoot him now. I ain't fixin' to tangle with that there Ashton's gunhawks. Are you?"

"You've got a point, there, Trav. Really you do. I'll go fetch that mule."

In less than an hour Tanaka Tom regained consciousness. He moaned softly and then willed himself to remain quiet. Slung like a bag of flour over the packsaddle of his mule the way he was, aching from the brutalizing given him by the bounty hunters, the trip was far from comfortable. To distract his mind and perhaps to give him a chance to devise a means of escape, the Six-gun Samurai let his thoughts wander back over his days in training as a warrior of Japan.

True courage lies in living when it is right to live and dying when it is right to die.

Think of death in the full knowledge of what honor demands . . .

Loyalty, a spirit of justice and bravery are the natural virtues of the samurai.

A samurai whose only attribute is strength is not acceptable. He must use his leisure time to practice poetry and understand the tea ceremony, not to mention the necessity of science studies.

So read the wisdom of the code of *Bushido*, the *Budo Shoshin Shu*, drawn up in the seventeenth century by Daidoji Yuzan. A way of living and a way of dying. To many, Tom realized, an overly simplistic view of life,

110

but to a samurai, it represented all that was necessary. At least until 1868 and the end of the shogunate. From the succession of the Emperor Meiji, the warrior class had been on the way out. Except for those immediately connected to the court, and the regiments they commanded, the samurai had reached their twilight. It did not, however, change the thinking patterns of the individual samurai, ingrained since childhood.

Escape, the samurai were taught, could always be effected unless one sustained a killing wound. Surrender to an enemy was unthinkable, dishonorable. He had been captured, so he must escape. The ultimate escape, if that became necessary, could come through biting off his tongue and bleeding to death. First, though, came thoughts of freedom and revenge on the enemy. Tom let his mind dwell on that until the bounty hunters halted for the night.

Cold wetness touched the back of Tom's head and bound hands and, in the glimmer of twilight, he raised his eyes to see snow falling while Clive Niebocker dragged him from the packsaddle. Such a storm, he calculated, would provide the ideal time for him to make his break. All he need do was wait.

Chapter Fourteen

"Dang-busted snow," Clive Niebocker griped while he gathered fallen branches for firewood. "It makes a feller want to make camp on the fringes of hell just to get away from the awful stuff."

"Quit yer complainin', Clive. Within three days we'll have collected our money by wire and be on our way to San Francisco on the train." Travis McNee turned back to his chore of building a fire, his mind already spending his share of the reward, minus that sent to his wife of course, on the silken lovelies in several of the bordellos on the 'Frisco waterfront. Neither man paid the least attention to their captive.

Tom Fletcher lay where he'd been dumped, against the bole of a rough-barked pine. His hands had been tied behind him, yet proved no handicap when he began tugging at the narrow *obi* sash around his waist. He pulled on the cloth with patient stealth until his fingers closed over the lacquered wooden case that contained his eating utensils; a pair of ivory chopsticks and a small knife, along with his personal calligraph, his "chop" mark. Tanaka Tom extracted the slender box from its place in the girdle and eased himself back. Now he needed only to wait for a proper opportunity. Flame crackled among the broken branches and McNee left the fire to get a blackened granite coffee pot, a cast-iron skillet and a greasy slab of nearly rancid bacon.

"Ain't we far enough away now to finish him off?"

"For Christ's sake, Clive. I'm cold and wet and hungry. It can wait until tomorrow. He ain't goin' nowhere."

"Whatever you say, Trav, whatever you say."

McNee sliced thick hunks of the bacon into the skillet, cooked it to a soft, underdone transparency. Then he hacked a potato into bits and fried them in the grease. By then the coffee had boiled long enough. He and Clive ate, slobbering over their food and noisily licking grease from their fingers. From the look and smell of the viands, Tanaka Tom didn't mind the least not being offered any. Half an hour later, McNee built up the fire and the two bounty hunters, after briefly checking the ropes securing Tom, rolled into their blankets near the blaze. They soon fell into grunting, snoring slumber.

Tanaka Tom listened intently to their sleep sounds, eyes straining in the firelight. Total darkness had come with the snowstorm and outside the circle of brightness from the flickering flames, not even the large, wet flakes could be seen falling endlessly to pile up on the ground. Carefully Tom drew the slender blade from its sheath and began sawing at the resin-toughened strand of rope wrapped around his wrists.

The keen edge of finely honed steel bit deeply so that in a few minutes, Tom felt his bonds part and circulation tingled painfully back into his hands. He waited another fifteen minutes, watching McNee and Niebocker, before cutting the line that spanned his chest, holding him to the tree trunk. Every nerve of his body clamored for him to hurry, to be up and out of this camp. With patience born of experience he resisted the urge, waited yet longer to be sure both of his enemies slept, before he bent forward and severed the cord around his ankles.

A soft pop accompanied the yielding of rope to knife and Tanaka Tom tensed, held himself motionless for several long, silent seconds. During that time Tom had a chance to think beyond the immediate plan of escape. He felt he shouldn't kill these men, they were some sort

of law officers with a warrant for his arrest. They had
nothing to do with Ashton or, for that matter, Colonel
Edward Hollister. He should, he decided, take thier
horses and his pack mule and ride out quietly. If they
did nothing to interfere with this, he'd let them both
live. With smooth, controlled movements of his body,
Tanaka Tom rose from the ground into a crouched posture and crept cautiously through the sleeping camp.

Clive Niebocker slept poorly. He hated the damp and
cold and snow. It reminded him of his wretched childhood on a worthless, unproductive homestead high on
the slopes of the Sierra Nevada in Northern California.
One of seven living children, Clive's belly always went
empty and, being the third in age, he frequently got the
blame for the failures of the others. By the time Clive
had reached ten years of age, his father had slid from
being an embittered dirt farmer down on his luck to a
vicious drunk. A year later, following a severe beating,
Clive ran away from home.

In the San Francisco of 1856 he found an entirely
different, though every bit as harsh, mode of life. For a
time he had been an inmate in a brothel that catered to
the perverse appetites of certain men. When he grew
older and lost his appeal to the clientele, he had been
cast out into the streets. There he learned to sap
drunken sailors and other unwary persons and roll them
for their money. He located and beat into compliance
several young girls, whom he enjoyed for a while then
sold into various cribs scattered along the waterfront
from Bay Street past the Embarcadero. At seventeen he
ran afoul of the law for beating up one of his girls who
had tried to escape from a bordello.

Clive fled to Arizona and from there drifted into
stage robbing. He swung east, to New Mexico Territory
for a while and hired out as a gunslick during some of
the early range wars, at last getting a price on his head
and, after killing the bounty hunter who tracked him
down, assumed that identity and went into the business.
His life in a desert climate had strengthened his dislike

of cold. Now he suffered from it like he had not experienced in years.

Cold air penetrated the blankets and brushed at Clive's spine, sending a shiver over him and awakening the bounty hunter. In that drowsy state between sleep and full wakefulness, he realized the fire had died down. Wrapping the blanket around him for its scant additional warmth, Clive rose and shuffled to the firewood pile. He clutched an armful of branches to his scrawny chest and turned back toward the bed of barely glowing embers. That's when he saw Tanaka Tom Fletcher.

Clive's mouth gaped in disbelief as Tom stopped in mid-stride, dropped the lead-rope to his pack mule and turned to the bulging packsaddle. In an instant Tanaka Tom spun around, a short length of shining steel, no broader than two finger widths, in one hand. Clive opened his mouth to shout a warning, but no sound came. The bounty man's mind could hardly take in what happened next.

Tanaka Tom seemed to float into the air, legs tucked up, sword arm extended, bent at the elbow, the keen edge of his *ho-tachi* pointed toward Clive. It rose in a graceful arc while fractions of a second seemed to lengthen into hours and Tom continued on his airborne course. Then suddenly time had meaning again as the small sword flashed downward.

Clive raised the bundle of sticks in a helpless attempt to ward off the descending steel, only to have it part in the middle, sliced through as surely and cleanly as his own chest and abdomen a pulse beat later. A feeling of fire and intense pain burned for a brief moment when Tom's *ho-tachi* cleaved through Clive's ribs, then continued to open flesh in a thin, surgically precise fine red line all the way to Clive's hip bone. His intestines spilled onto the ground, steam rising into the cold night air from the moist coils and emptying body cavity, and Clive died without uttering a sound. Tanaka Tom rushed to Travis McNee, weapon poised.

McNee lay in sodden slumber, an empty whisky bottle clutched in one outflung arm. His partner had met his death without disturbing McNee's liquor-induced sleep. Tom noted the helpless condition of the man, reversed his blade and smashed downward with the handle, to strike McNee behind the ear with the *kashira*. It insured McNee an even longer repose and a far worse headache. Tom quickly ran to the grazing horses.

He saddled one, untied them from the picket stakes and swung aboard. Leading his pack mule, driving the riderless animals before him, he rode out of camp.

Snow reached knee-high on the horses and they plowed through it with uneven, uncertain steps. More of the fat flakes were falling, the mount Tom had chosen grunted in discomfort as it struggled along. The Six-gun Samurai had no way of knowing for certain, but he realized he had a long ride ahead of him to reach Aspen Gap.

"Where has he gone?" Bradley Ashton thundered when Larry Don Saggerty brought him news of Tanaka Tom's disappearance. "How could he go anywhere in this wretched weather?"

"Seems as how he must have left before this storm set in. Nobody's seen him since right after the noonin'."

"How can that be? We have guards out, do we not? He . . . he must be on his way to warn the people of Aspen Gap."

"Awh, I wouldn't be so certain of that, Rev'ren' Ashton," the gunslinger contradicted his boss. "Might be he's a man of peace and hu . . . humili . . ."

"Humility," Ashton snapped.

"Right. Peace and humility like he said and the thought of shootin' up a town and all scared him off."

"Which makes him even more dangerous. He could tell others our identity."

"I didn't think this was any big secret. I mean, after all, how do you hide burnin' down a whole town?"

Ashton smiled condescendingly and replied as one does to a slow child. "We of New Caanaland will be the only survivors of that little fracus, Larry Don. Don't

116

you remember that? Surely that will make identifying the perpetrators a great deal more difficult?"

"I never thought of that. I guess you're right, boss."

"Which brings us back to our missing Brother Thomas. We must find him before the attack on Aspen Gap."

"We can't do either until this blizzard lets up. My calculatin' says that probably won't be until some time tomorrow."

"You might as well have my supper prepared then. Make it for two and send Margaret to me."

Yes, sir, Rev'ren'."

Tanaka Tom traveled for more than an hour in the darkness and windblown snow until he came to realize he'd been making a wide circle. He stopped and removed his hat, shaking it clear of a heavy accumulation of wet flakes. He studied the sky, vainly hoping for some glimmering that would indicate a lessening of the weather and the location of the moon. It suddenly came clear to him that he hadn't the least idea of direction. A samurai *couldn't get lost*, the nature of their training was supposed to keep them in perfect harmony with nature and attuned to the cardinal points, so the thought never expressed itself to him in that context.

"One good thing, though," Tom spoke his thoughts aloud. "This blizzard's sure to keep Ashton from carrying out his raid on Aspen Gap." Despite the delay forced upon him, he might have time to reach the town before hand. First things first, though. He had to find a place to hole-up until the storm ended. With a grunt he reined his horse hard to the left of his present course and started off in another direction.

With a sob of impatience, Margaret Dorn flung herself from her chair at the table, causing Bradley Ashton's hand to be withdrawn from the unbuttoned bodice of her dress where he'd been industriously caressing her right breast. She paced the floor with restless strides, her body charged with near-maniacal energy. At the

117

window she paused a moment, looking out at a heavy blanket of snow covering the ground while more fat white flakes fell from the black sky. She turned away with an angry rustle of cloth and her words crackled with frustration.

"Ooooh, this infernal weather! I can't tolerate this horrible weather!"

"There's really very little we can do about it, my dear."

"You could try praying it away," Margaret purred with cynical malice.

"Don't be nasty, dear Margaret. We have such a pleasant night ahead of us."

"Not tonight. I . . . I don't feel like it." With a start, Margaret discovered that what she'd said was true. Not for the first time lately she found herself with less than burning desire to have this man's huge member thrusting deep inside her body.

"Very well," Ashton returned coolly. He drained the last of a large glass of brandy and sat it aside. "I could use a little variety. Why don't you fetch me one of those dear little ones from the Sacred Sisterhood. I think a . . . ah, redhead would intrigue me most."

Helen Blair! A sudden chill passed through Margaret Dorn at the thought of the twelve-year-old's name. Bradley had summoned the little bitch three times during the several weeks since Helen's initiation. He'd kept her with him four days at the time, she recalled with anger. Margaret felt the grip of icy panic as she faced the frightful possibility that she might be replaced by a younger girl.

No! Not after all her plannning and scheming. She saw herself coming out of this a rich and powerful woman. When Ashton finally folded his little tent show and left here a wealthy man, Margaret intended to go along. No snot-nosed little brat with a hot and willing cleft between her legs would take that away from her. She would not have her body used by Ashton and then cast aside to be rutted upon by those coarse deacons when she reached maturity, like she'd seen happen to some of the others when they came to an age of seventeen or so and no longer held an attraction for Bradley Ashton. No, not Margaret Dorn. She was too clever even for the crafty little preacher. No matter what happened to the others, to Ashton himself, she was going to make this time in her life pay and pay well. To do so meant to keep her position and that meant dealing with Helen Blair.

She knew what Helen liked, what excited her. A small smile played about her pouting mouth. She also knew what the little girl didn't enjoy. And none of the others were more practiced in that art than she. Her plan fully formed, she turned a sweet countenance on Bradley Ashton.

"If you really want variety, why not take us both to your bed? Something decidedly different, no?"

Newly awakened passion flamed in Bradley Ashton's eyes. "Yes. Let's do that. An unusual . . . and exciting difference indeed."

For the first time in her life, Helen Blair felt frightened. Oh, she'd been scared enough when she reported for her initiation into the Sacred Sisters, yet that had been nothing like this. She hadn't minded *that* much at all, enjoyed it in fact, those four wonderful days, like the other three times she was later summoned to serve the Reverend Master. But knowing what lay ahead of her, and recalling what had just happened, she felt dirty and terrified at the same time.

Trembling, she clutched a sharp kitchen knife to her breast under her robes as she walked through the snow alongside a still-aroused Margaret Dorn and climbed the dirt-covered steps to the parsonage.

Chapter Fifteen

"The little bitch cut me!" Bradley Ashton's voice came out a terror-toned soprano. *How could any of my sweet Little Sisters do such a thing?* his mind clamored at him. He looked in fright across the room to where Margaret stood at the bedroom window. Her one hand frantically clutched the heavy velvet draperies while she screamed hysterically.

"Help! Murderer! We're being murdered! Help!" Her other hand gingerly supported the blood-slimed handle of the kitchen knife, buried nearly to the hilt in her shoulder, bracing it to prevent painful movement.

Ashton's face paled when his fingertips encountered the trickle of blood down his side from the searing, throbbing slash along his ribs. This was a reality that couldn't be denied. But Helen doing it? Little Helen? His mind wanted to reject the possibility.

She'd come trembling to her initiation, a nervous virgin. After that, it had been different, though. Her performance had, much to his surprise, excelled even that of the insatiable Margaret. So wondrously inventive had they been together that he had not once thought of the whips and leather hoods, the braided rawhide thongs and pliable, glove-soft hip boots Margaret had recommended for this night's entertainment. He couldn't believe it had happened. Yet, his pain left no doubt, nor, when he looked down, could he help but see the verity of it lying before him.

Helen Blair lay sprawled naked on the bedroom

floor. A large red weal spread across her cheek, under the left eye, and a thin line of blood ran from one nostril. He had hit her hard, knocking her unconscious after she had stabbed Margaret. Yes, Margaret. She'd begun to wear thin lately, her constant assertion of authority and seemingly purposeless persecution of her little brother. The possibility that he would not have his present problems except for her had occurred to him and he had, only that day, decided to replace her with Helen. Now all that had been ruined. How? Why? Shock and surprise began to wear off and the pain set in with greater intensity, bringing a moan from Ashton's lips.

"What th' hell happened, boss? . . . Hunnnh?" Larry Don Saggerty charged into the room, gun in hand, stumbling over the supine form of Helen Blair. He quickly took in the naked child, blood and wounds, the knife and the tight-lipped, pain-filled expression on Margaret's face.

"S-she t-t-tried to kill us both," Ashton blurted out. "Stabbing and slashing with that knife." Ashton pointed to where Margaret stood. She no longer screamed, but her eyes were dark vessels of horror. She seemed oblivious to her surroundings. As though he only now discovered their nudity, Ashton reached for his dressing gown, addressing his words to Margaret as he slid into the robe. "Let me cover you, Margaret, my dear."

"I told you that messin' around with them little kids would bring you nothin' but trouble. Didn't I, boss?"

"Keep your opinions to yourself, *Mister* Saggerty. Send Joe in here with hot water to help with our wounds. And get this . . . this monster out of here. Lock her in the detention cell until I decide what to do with her." Ashton walked to where Margaret stood and gently placed her robe about her shoulders. In two minutes Joe arrived with a large basin of hot water and an armload of towels. Ashton set about tending their injuries.

"This is going to hurt some, my dear, but that knife has to come out." Ashton felt Margaret tense under his

121

fingers. He wrapped one hand around the wooden slab handle and jerked the blade from her flesh. Margaret shrieked once, pitifully, and passed out. Ashton caught her in his arms, lifted her effortlessly and carried her to the bed.

"That's a blessin', boss," Joe, his faithful house servant, opined. "It'll make our work easier."

Behind them, Larry Don had returned. He covered Helen with her white Sisterhood robe, picked her up in his arms and quietly left the room. Ignoring his chief enforcer, Ashton continued to rant against disobedience.

"It's those Miller girls, I tell you."

"Wha-what is?" Margaret regained consciousness while Ashton worked to dress her wound.

"The sins of willfulness and disobedience are spreading through New Caanaland like the plague through Europe. It's the fault of those damned Miller girls. Yes, and your brother, Jamie, and your parents. My eyes have been opened to what you warned of, my dear. Taking it in their heads to leave here, all of them. They did it to hurt us, to undermine authority in New Caanaland. Once such seeds of rebellion are cast abroad, little can be done to stop their rapid growth. They must be made to pay before those seeds can germinate."

Despite her pain, Margaret felt a surge of exaltant triumph. "Yes, dear Bradley, yes. And Helen Blair most of all. She must be made to suffer horribly for what she's done to us."

"They'll all get the same. The stake, by the Almighty, the stake!"

"Perfect. Let them all burn for their sins and that will stop any defiance of our authority among the others."

Eyes ablaze with madness and hatred, Bradley Ashton relished the punishment he'd decreed. "We ride for Aspen Gap in the morning. No quarter given to the heretics. We shall return here in glory to mete out punishment on the transgressors. Let them die at the stake!"

* * *

Dawn came to a landscape of featureless white, yet the sun still held the last warmth of the waning summer. Slowly, at first, the hoary coating on leaves and branches began to melt and fall to the ground with hushed plops, the drifts across the road slagging down, leaving a clearly defined, trough-like wallow of mud. Tanaka Tom Fletcher awakened to this world no more sure of his location than during the height of the blizzard.

With the coming of full daylight Tom found he had taken shelter in an abandoned building that had once served as a bunkhouse for a mining operation. Logic dictated that the rutted, slippery trail would eventually lead to a main road and civilization, so after a brief breakfast of tea and cold biscuit, the Six-gun Samurai rode out on the late Clive Niebocker's horse, drawing his pack mule behind.

At the bottom of the second long grade he had been compelled to climb then slither down in the greasy mud formed by melting snow, Tanaka Tom found the main road. A crudely made wooden sign, the letters hand-carved, indicated the way:

ASPEN GAP—14 miles
GRANITE—47 miles

Tom turned to the right and headed at a fast trot toward Aspen Gap. At his present rate of travel, on a bad road, he knew he wouldn't make town much before noon. Ashton would have farther to go, but would he have waited until daylight? Whatever the case, he had no control over the mad preacher's movements. Tanaka Tom put the unsolvable problem behind him and urged more speed out of the strange horse.

At half-past twelve that afternoon, tired, mud-splattered and hungry, Tom Fletcher tied Niebocker's horse to the hitch rail outside the sheriff's office and jail. He located the lawdog in the Owl Car cafe down the street and, after washing away some of the trail's damage, accepted a chair at the same table and ordered

123

a meal. While the two men waited for their food to be delivered, Tom explained his mission.

"I can see by your face that you are not believing this," Tom concluded. "It is entirely true. Ashton has lost his reason and intends to attack this town. I am not accustomed to having my word questioned. I can take full responsibility for organizing a defense of Aspen Gap. That way, if I am wrong, no blame shall fall on you and I have my own way to atone for it." Tom didn't mention the ritual suicide of *seppuku* to the sheriff in detail, but the deep earnestness of his voice changed the lawman's expression.

"I can't believe it. Only a crazy man would attack a town. I allow that gettin' someone to defend it is even less likely. There aren't that many men of fightin' age around these parts. When the mines played out, most of the healthy young ones headed for better pickin's. What we got mostly is gray-beards and sprats under sixteen or so. But if you're right, somethin' oughtta be done. And if you're willin' to stake your repe'tation on it, I suppose the least I can do is give you a chance."

"How can we gather them all together so I can explain and organize them?"

"I suppose the fire bell would be best. Everybody turns out for that." The sheriff looked up and saw the waitress headed their way with a tray filled with steaming food. "Let's eat up first then go take care of that very thing."

Forty minutes later the strident clanging of a blacksmith's hammer against the huge steel rim of an ore wagon wheel hung outside the firehouse summoned the male population of Aspen Gap. They came at a run, stripping out of coats and vests, preparing to do battle with the flames.

"Where's the fire, Harvey?" the baker asked, his flour-whitened face emphasizing the largeness of his black eyes.

"No fire, George. When everyone gets here, I want you to listen up to this gentleman here." In another pair of minutes the sheriff indicated that all had assembled, including a gaggle of excited, babbling, barefoot boys.

"This here's Tom Fletcher. I think y'all know him from the other day when he brought in those folks who escaped from New Caanaland. He's got somethin' important to say. Mr. Fletcher."

"Thank you, Sheriff. I have just come from Ashton's town at Yellow Creek, this New Caanaland. Ashton is planning to send an armed force against Aspen Gap." A chorus of consternation and disbelief rose from the assembled group. "I'm serious, men. Listen to me. Ashton uses a powerful Indian drug to poison the minds of his congregation. When they are under its influence, he can make them do anything he wants. Last night's blizzard may have prevented their starting for here, but they are coming and they can be here at any moment now. Go get your guns, every man and boy over fourteen, and meet back here in five minutes."

Tom hadn't given the men an opportunity to protest or question. In silence they turned their heads toward Sheriff Weller. At a curt, "Do what he says," from the lawman, they walked off without another word to fetch their weapons. That left behind only Weller and Tom and the band of wide-eyed, excited boys.

"Hey, Mister. I can shoot, too. I even got my own gun," a runty, black-haired boy of thirteen or so piped up in a voice that cracked occasionally with approaching manhood. "So can these fellers," he concluded, indicating half a dozen others who grouped around him.

Tom examined the lads for a long, sober moment, then made his decision. "All right. Go get your guns. You can be our second line of defense, right here in town."

"Huh!" the starled youngster exploded. "Ain't you gonna defend the town?"

A smile creased Tom's mouth. "We are, but I intend to make it easy for all of us." Tom's plans formed effortlessly in his mind as he talked. "We're going to meet Ashton in the open where he hasn't the advantage of buildings to interrupt our field of fire. Now get along, scoot."

When the men returned, Tnaka Tom quickly organized them. "The creek that runs north and south right outside town makes a natural line of defense. The bridge over it is narrow enough to make a death trap for anyone trying to rush it. Let's haul wagons loaded with hay bales and sacks of grain out and form a line on this side of the creek, about fifty feet back. We'll force them to leave the road, come at us across open country. When they ford the creek and climb the near bank they will be nearly helpless. Concentrated fire will stop them cold.

"Now, how many of you have had army service?" Tom looked at the collection of men. The sheriff had not understated his appraisal. Most were in their fifties, a few younger, then a wide gap in age to the youngsters. Several men raised their hands in response to the Six-gun Samurai's question.

Tom picked the three who held their weapons the most competently, counting the total. Forty-five men, including the youths, armed with a variety of shotguns, single shot and repeating rifles, a few revolvers. Tom quickly made his order of battle, pointing out his picked men.

"You three will command a group of nine each. I will take the center with fifteen. Don't divide yourselves so all of the shotguns are in one place. Mix it up so there are some repeating rifles, shotguns and single shot guns in each group. Everyone hold fire until I give the command from this end of the bridge. We want them well in range and committed so they can not circle around us and take the town from the rear. Whenever possible, shoot for the horses. On foot they will be helpless."

"Horse killin's a serious matter around here, Mister," the livery stable owner advised.

"Dying and having your town burned down around your ears is a great deal more serious, isn't it?" Tanaka Tom countered in a quiet voice. A ripple of laughter went through the crowd. The door for further comment had been opened though.

126

"I thought you said only boys over fourteen," George, the baker, complained. "Bobby Tucker there ain't but twelve."

"I'll be thirteen next month," the black-haired boy grumbled through a pout.

"Bobby and these other boys all say they want to help and that they can shoot as good as any man. I'm making them our second line of defense. They are to take up places that give cover but have a commanding view of the main street. In the event any of Ashton's army breaks through our lines, it will be their job to stop those men before they do any damage and hold them until we can deal with the threat."

"But these are just children, boys of eleven and twelve."

"George is it? George, I fought my first battle, against pirates, at thirteen. I killed two men who were trying to grab my horse with a sword not three feet long. These guns will give the boys a considerable advantage in distance from danger over that sword, don't you think?"

Unexpected support came from Sheriff Weller. "Bobby here can take the eye out of a squirrel at fifty yards. Can you do as well, George?" He reached out and affectionately ruffled the boy's thick mop of hair.

"Well, now, Harv . . . ah, it ain't that exactly. It's . . . well, his Maw's a widder woman an' all and what would happen if he got kilt?"

"I ain't afraid of gettin' hurt, Mr. Jones. None of us is." Bobby puffed out his chest to show his bravery. "My Maw sent me with her blessin' and she's goin' to the church to light candles for all of us. An' Father Moffitt sent along his ol' Navy Colt for a back-up gun."

Harvey Weller chuckled deep in his throat. "I guess that settles it, then, George. With the Lord and Father Moffitt on the lad's side, he's pretty well fixed . . . we all are."

"Let's get moving," Tom commanded, taking the initiative away from the baker. "Roll those wagons into position and everyone take a place behind them. I'll be by to check on your work."

Early evening came and still no sign of Ashton's zealot army. Tom Fletcher had closely observed the setting of Aspen Gap's defenses and made occasional suggestions to strengthen them. He drilled the volunteer soldiers on volley fire as an opener to battle, discussed how men could pick individual targets without wasting ammunition on a single man. The simplicity of it, an old samurai tactic, of assigning individual fields of responsibility, with no one firing on any target outside his own area, had amazed the men. It had been something unknown even to the Civil War veterans. Some of the boy volunteers had been assigned to work as ammunition runners between the gunsmithy and general store and the defensive works. Satisfied at last, Tom released half of the men to go eat an early supper in rotation with those on guard and, as the sun slipped toward the western peaks, went himself to take a meal.

At a quarter past six, while Tom finished an order of boiled rice and a brace of tender, perfectly broiled trout, he realized he had not even taken time to check on the Miller girls, or to warn them of Ashton's intentions. He cleaned his plate hastily and strode out of the cafe, on his way to Maw Tamblin's boarding house.

Tanaka Tom found Rachel in the kitchen helping Maw Tamblin clean up after the evening meal. The girl seemed happy and bright, an entirely different child from the one he had led away from New Caanaland. He quickly explained the situation and possible danger to the girls.

"I heard the fuss and bother uptown," Maw Tamblin commented, wiping a large serving platter. "Never figured that horrid man would try somethin' so all-fired crazy as this, though. I'll load up my late husband's shotgun and keep an eye peeled. Earl, God rest his soul, taught me to shoot when I was only a girl new-married. I still am, if I do say so myself, a fair good shot."

"I'll trust them in your care, then," Tom replied tactfully, making his exit. "Is Martha up in her room?"

"Sure enough. Though I'll wager she'll be burned you didn't come visitin' straight off you got back." Maw Tamblin whooped gleefully at her own observation while Tom ducked his head in farewell and hurried from the kitchen.

"Oh, Tom, Tom!" Martha cried when she looked up to see him standing in the open doorway. She rushed to him and threw her arms about his neck, covering his face with kisses. "I was so worried about you. And . . . and the most horrible thing happened while you were gone."

"What was that, Martha-*san?*" Tom was surprised to discover he had a deep concern that went beyond worry over the two girls' welfare and safety.

"It's . . . over now. Why, I've nearly forgotten all about it now, with you here."

"Tell me about it anyway." A hard note crept into Tom's voice, evidence of his worry.

"It has nothing to do with Rev . . . ah, Ashton. Really it . . ." she saw the glint in Tom's eye and went on. "I was taken captive by two men. They were hunting you. They said all sorts of awful things about you and . . . and threatened to rape me if I didn't tell them where you had gone. I . . . oh, my darling, I am so ashamed, so dismally weak and ashamed. I . . . I told them you'd gone to New Caanaland."

"Those bounty hunters. Yes. That figures." Tom was unaware he had spoken aloud until he saw the widening of Martha's eyes and the manner in which she pressed both hands to her mouth. "It is all right, Martha-*san.* I had an encounter with them. They will give us no more trouble."

"H-how can you be so sure?"

Tom sought to avoid the subject. "Tell me, did you inform the sheriff about what happened?"

"Yes, of course," she lied to conceal her promise to McNee.

"Then he won't be coming around town, we can be sure of that."

"He? There were two of them, Tom."

"I know. One of them . . . died . . . when I escaped from them."

"I . . . see." Realization that Tom had yet more blood on his hands caused Martha to change the subject. "What is all that excitement uptown about?"

As she led the way to a settle in the bay window, Tom told her, sparing none of the details. He noted, also, that she had firmly closed and latched the door. The smallness of the loveseat put Martha almost in his lap and she listened wide-eyed to his recital. When he finished she pressed against him, kissing with a fervency he quickly returned. Her fingers flew to Tom's shirt-front, fumbling with the buttons, her small, warm hand entering to caress this naked chest. Her other arm encircled his neck, drawing his lips tightly against hers and her tongue probed inside his mouth.

When their kiss ended, Martha swayed away from him, both hands flying to the back of her neck, pulling at ribbons and buttons, letting the cloth fall about her waist. Then she came into his arms again, their mouths hungry, demanding. Tom felt himself stiffening in eager response and Martha twisted away from him with a frenzied cry, rose and slid out of her dress to stand before him in her shift.

Tom lifted her in his arms and carried her to the bed. With panting urgency they hurriedly removed their clothing, Martha releasing small mews of desire as she struggled with a stubborn hook. Martha gave forth a moan of delight as her fluttering fingers exposed Tom's tumescent, pendulous manhood and she fell backward on the bed. Gently Tom entered her, thrusting deeply. Slowly, languorously they made love, conscious of their need to keep silent so as not to betray their activity to those outside the room.

When at last they climbed to the peak and shuddered over it into blissful, trembling climax, Tanaka Tom lay beside the girl in her rumpled bed. Martha reached out

130

with her warm, damp fingers and delicately traced a line along Tom's burning flesh, down over the flat, hard muscles of his abdomen, halting to circle the indented ridge that surrounded his navel, then onward to the base of his flaccid organ, to close about it possessively.

"You know," she whispered in a distant, little girl voice, "everytime I see that huge part of you and feel it driving deep inside me I could simply die of happiness."

Tanaka Tom chuckled deep in his throat. "It is a sword that seldom draws blood and never kills." His lips pursed and his brow puckered in concentration. "Listen to this:

> *Spring-like, my sword, trust well and true,*
> *Kills not, wounds not,*
> *Quickening new life.*"

"Ooooooh! You awful man! That's dirty," Martha cried, squeezing the flesh in her grasp.

"No it's not. It's a poem, a *haiku*. *Haiku's* are only made to describe some beautiful thought or scene or event in a samurai's life."

"What I mean is, we'd better not be quickening new life." She paused a moment, her face turning impish. "Though I wouldn't really mind much, knowing he was yours."

"You're certain it would be a *he*?"

"Coming from you, there could be no other way." She reared up then and kissed Tom wetly, passionately, then broke off with a gasp. "Oooh. Something seems to be quickening with life of its own," she observed, straddling him, drawing back his foreskin and positioning herself to receive Tom's ready flesh a second time.

Faster now they joined their efforts, working deliriously to the pinnacle of mutual, joyful release. They lay back in a tangle of arms and legs, still joined at their tender parts, wrapped in sweaty contentment for some ten long, silent minutes. Amazingly, then, with

131

Martha's eager assistance, Tom found himself being roused for a third effort. At that precise second the strident clanging of the fire bell invaded the room through a partly open window.

Ashton's army of religious fanatics had arrived to do battle.

Chapter Sixteen

With a rush of energy Tanaka Tom tried to finish them both, but found he could not. The call to combat clamored too loudly in his ear. He climbed from the bed and dressed. Aching and unfulfilled, Martha cried out her need to him. He kissed her briefly and left the room.

Men already streamed from doorways all down the street when Tom reached the tie-rail and loosened the reins of his Morgan. He rode swiftly to the edge of town and checked with each of his appointed subordinates.

"There they are, Fletcher," George Jones told Tom, pointing to a cluster of figures reined up some hundred yards beyond the other side of the creek. "They saw us forted up like this and hauled up short. You reckon they'll be crazy enough to go through with it?"

"Ashton is . . . and that's all it takes." Tom left the baker with that thought and rode on to check his other two leaders. They showed him their dispositions of troops and ammunition and expressed their anxiousness to fight. Tom praised their efforts and went to his place at the bridge.

Images of samurai battle formations and tactics filled his head and Tom thought of ways to translate them into use here. His memory sight showed him ranks of archers lined up, their great, eight-foot long *kyos* raised, strings forming wide mouthed Vees, arrows poised. Then the release, not a spoken command, but a simultaneous loosing of the shafts when each follower of *kyudo* "knows" it is the precise moment to let fly. The sky fills with a cloud of feathered death, the volley falling on the heads of the enemy. Nodding his satisfaction, Tom passed the word left and right to remind the men to fire at least two volleys during the initial charge before picking targets of opportunity. Tanaka Tom had taken time during the day to fully arm himself and now he drew his Winchester. From the distance, thin and reedy, Ashton's voice came to him.

"Oh, Lord of Hosts, grant us the strength to vanquish the armies of Satan. Into the breach, men. Make way! In the name of the Almighty, submit or die!"

The would-be conquerors of Aspen Gap humped their horses into a gallop and thundered down on the bridge. Tanaka Tom sighted in on the exact center of the span, waiting for a target. His peripheral vision, like that of any good commander, had widened so that his eyes could take in as much of the battlefront as possible.

Several of the riders, he saw, recognized the folly of trying to carry the bridge. They reined to the sides, spreading out into a line to left and right, charging the creekbank. Ashton lagged behind in the center, others gaining first positions on the wooden planks. Tom's sights centered on one man's chest and his finger squeezed on the trigger.

The Winchester barked, its detonation lost in a ragged volley that spread from the center to each flank of the Six-gun Samurai's line. Over his sights Tanaka Tom saw the charging gunslinger smashed backward, then pitch to the front, over his saddlehorn and under the pounding hooves of the mounts behind him. Several horses crashed to the ground, shrieking in pain, and as a second volley sounded, the first charge ended as quickly as it began.

The men of Aspen Gap kept up sporadic fire as the stragglers withdrew. When the last ones rode or stumbled out of range, quiet held. In the dim twilight, Ashton's voice, but not his words, could be heard exhorting

134

his men. Then yellow ribbons of flame flickered in the growing darkness, the raiders lighting torches. Amid ringing cries of defiance, the second charge launched against the defenders.

This time they avoided bunching up near the bridge, swinging wide toward the flanks. When they reached the proper range, another volley whipped into them, horses and men shrieking, the sweet stench of blood and death filling the air with the dust. Once more the attackers were beaten off, yet several more than before reached the creek, crossed it and surged up the near bank. Most of those fell to shotgun blasts, while two of their ranks wound through into the rear of the defenders, torches sputtering above their heads. Tanaka Tom whirled his Morgan stallion and galloped toward the pair, shoving his Winchester into its scabbard and drawing his *katana*. The finely honed, superbly forged steel glinted in the waning light as he closed with the first raider. The blade whistled through the air and Loren Greun shrieked in horrified agony when he recognized the once "humble" Brother Thomas an instant before his body got sliced in half an inch above his navel.

The upper portion of the corpse fell from its place into the dust while the panicked horse raced on into the streets of Aspen Gap, trailing long strands of Loren's intestines. Tanaka Tom reared and whirled the Morgan and thundered down on his second opponent. He watched helplessly while the rider whirled his torch in great arcs around his head and then threw it through a second-floor window of the general mercantile store. He didn't get to admire his handiwork, though.

In the same second of release, Tanaka Tom rode up to Jake Skagen and dropped the point of his sword level so that the slanted tip of the *katana* slid easily into the man's throat in a *tsugi* thrust. With a flick of Tom's wrist, it cut outward, bringing with it a twin fountain of blood that washed up over the dying gunslinger's face and dripped off the brim of his hat. Jake made a croaking, airy sound through his second mouth and tumbled

135

from the saddle. Observing the arrival of fire fighters, Tanaka Tom returned to the front line.

"Think they'll try it a third time?" George Jones asked Tom when the Six-gun Samurai rode along inspecting the men defending the wagon barricade.

"I'm not sure. All we can do is wait and see."

Bradley Ashton drew his surviving fighting men farther out of the line of fire, stopping beyond a small rise in the ground where they could not be observed. He made a quick count, noting several wounded but able fighters mixed in with the other powder-smudged faces anxiously watching him.

"We're going to have to flank them if we have any hope of taking the town," Ashton informed them. "And remember why we're here. Of first importance is apprehending the Miller girls and spiriting them out of town to take back to New Caanaland. In that we must be successful if in nothing else."

"How we gonna do that? They're shootin' hell outta us, Rev'ren'," Larry Don protested.

"Larry Don, I want you to take five good men, none of the congregation, only deacons. We know the Millers are at this Maw Tamblin's boarding house. Now, we're all going to shift over, come at 'em through those trees on the north end of their line. We're going to try to turn their flank and get enough men on the other bank to do some good. That will also serve as a diversion for you."

Despite his unstable mind, Bradley Ashton had been a competent officer in the 251st Ohio, leading his men well and displaying an extraordinary grasp of the intricacies of tactics. Although he later grew to hate his soldiering years, this talent came back to him now, in the moment of his greatest need.

"You're to ride even further out, Larry Don, circling town and coming in by the east road. Go directly to Maw Tamblin's and get those girls. Meanwhile we will be making a frontal attack on their left flank. You, you, you, and you," Ashton pointed out some fifteen of the farmers-turned-troopers in his zealot-army and three of his gunslinger-deacons. "I want you to remain on this side of the ridge, in reserve. Keep a lookout over on the other slope.

When we start to turn their flank, charge, and don't take time to fight those in the defensive works. Go right on through, into town and start burning down every building, shoot everyone who runs out. Once we've breached their lines, we'll join you and the job will be done. We can ride out to the east, circle wide and head back to New Caanaland. Any questions?"

"Uh . . ." one of the faithful asked, unsure of himself. "What if we don't do this what you're talkin' about, Rev'ren, Master, this turnin' their flank?"

"Why, the Almighty is on our side, Brother Jacob. We *will* prevail. Have faith and all things are possible. Everyone ready now? Then move out."

Martha Miller still lay nude on her bed, feeling bathed in the rosy warmth of total sexual fulfillment. After Tom had left, she stood before the mirror, stretching herself in different poses, running her hands over the slender length of her body, proud of the upthrust of her young breasts. Her heart still pounded and her inner being longed for the closeness of her lover. She returned, weak-kneed, to her damp and rumpled sheets to find solace in tears, as had legions of women before her when their men went off to war. Now the sounds of battle reached her from the distance, rousing her from her lethargic joy. A few shots, followed by a furious volley, sounded clearly, then more scattered reports and a ragged cheer.

Ashton's mob must have been turned back again, she thought. How horrible if the men couldn't hold him. She shuddered at the contemplation of such a fate. The door opened and Rachel entered in a rush. She stopped in midroom.

"Aaaam. I know what you two were doin," Martha's younger sister said teasingly. Rachel remained on the hook rug in the center of the floor, fists on her hips. Then she giggled. "Was it fun?"

"You nasty, monstrous little child!" Martha gasped, scandalized. "What put such dirty thoughts in your head?"

"Lisa and Helen and Kathy told me about what happened at their initiation into the Sacred Sisters, remember? Only they said it hurt a lot and wasn't much fun. You look sort of secret-happylike when you went on that picnic with Mr. Tom Fletcher. Did something happen then, too?"

"I ought to slap your sassy face around on the other side of your head for that, Miss Rachel Miller. It's none of your business what Mr. Fletcher and I do. We have our . . . secrets."

"You'd better put some clothes on, then, before Maw Tamblin finds out all about your . . . secrets," Rachel gloated, then clapped her hands together in front of her chest, forming two humped backs.

Suddenly both girls found themselves giggling together until Martha brought herself up short. "Say. I thought you didn't know about all that. That you hated the very thought of it and were afraid. That's why you wanted to get away from New Caanaland."

Rachel looked solemnly wise, a teasing glint in her eyes. "I didn't say I was afraid of *doing* it. Only that I was afraid of *him* and of *him* being the first one."

Peals of laughter came from both of them then. Martha climbed from the bed and slid into her shift, collecting her long black stockings, dress and button shoes, starting to dress. From outside the rattle of gunfire ominously increased in volume. Rachel dashed across the floor to her sister, hugging her desperately about the waist, a lonely, frightened child again.

"Oh, Martha, I'm so afraid. I'm scared they will come and get us and take me back to that awful Reverend Ashton. I . . . I want to save m-myself for the man I love . . . like you and your Mr. Tom, not that ugly old toad. Oh, please say they won't come."

At that same moment, before Martha could reply with reassurance for her frightened little sister, the waning light of evening blanked out in their window, ob-

138

scured by a huge form. A booted foot kicked in the glass and a man entered, followed by two more.

One of the intruders grabbed Rachel away from her elder sister, silencing her with a cloth stuffed in her open mouth, while the leader and another man clutched at Martha's struggling limbs. Larry Don Saggerty clapped one hamlike hand over Martha's mouth, shutting off the scream rising in her throat.

Chapter Seventeen

Tanaka Tom Fletcher saw the flanking attack developing before it hit the line and knew the consequences were it to be allowed to succeed. Brandishing his *katana*, he drew ten men from his center position and five from the first on his left, leading them to the threatened position.

"Form up along here, the Six-gun Samurai commanded, indicating that the first five townsmen reinforce George Jones's squad while the remainder spread out at a right angle. The right flank now took on a "L" shape, its bristling weapons delivering a high volume of accurate fire.

Although many of Ashton's zealots fell to that deadly scythe of bullets, they persisted, pushing hard against the reinforced flank. Gradually, though, they began to give ground as their losses mounted. When they at last pulled back, the corpses of five men and eleven horses littered the ground. Heartened by their success under great pressure, the men in the defenses raised a cheer. Tanaka Tom rode along the line, giving encouragement and correcting weak points.

"They gonna run now, I betcha," the burly blacksmith called out to Tom while a friend bandaged a bullet crease along the ironmonger's left arm.

"I wouldn't be certain of that. Honor demands at least another attack."

"Their *honor*? Where you get such funny notions, Mister?"

Tom didn't answer, going instead to check on casualties. Two men had been seriously wounded and carried back into town for the doctor to work on. One man lay huddled and hushed by death. A lad of fourteen had a bullet hole through the loose flesh of his right thigh, a clean wound that pierced both sides. He loudly insisted on staying, if someone would only get him a chair. Tom moved on, feeling satisfied with their high spirits. Then Ashton launched his next assault.

The attack again came against the flank. So swiftly did the riders from New Caanaland appear at the far end of the line that Tom had no time to reposition his mobile reserve. Three of the defenders fell, screaming in agony and half a dozen men broke through, torches flaring, headed for the center of town. Tom heard scattered gunfire coming from that direction a moment before he wheeled his Morgan and raced after the invaders.

Tanaka Tom closed with the rearmost gunman, delivering a stroke that slashed the man to his shoulder blades. He screamed and fell from his horse. Tom rode on, moving in on another as he saw the two in the lead jerk in their saddles and fall, clutching their chests. His second line of defense had wasted no time in coming into action. Tom reversed his sword and used the pommel to knock a lad of fifteen or so to the ground. He quickly whirled to locate the remaining enemy.

His rapid turn caused Tom's Morgan to crash into a fallen horse. The impact brought the sturdy animal to his knees, dislodging Tom, who rolled free and came up with his *katana* at the ready. He immediately raced after the remaining pair, who were throwing firebrands into buildings along the street. They spun their horses, drew rifles and dashed back down the street toward Tom.

Tom stopped, prepared to meet their charge, then stumbled awkwardly to one side, a powerful, agonizing pain blossoming in his head. A bullet, fired from behind him by Latigo Crowell, cut a deep gouge along the side of his head above his left ear, driving him to his knees. Tom felt a wash of warm, sticky wetness and blood flowed freely. He reached up to examine the wound, then toppled into the dusty street, while blackness yawned like a deep and bitter well.

Tanaka Tom awakened to a confusion of voices. Loudest was that of Sheriff Harvey Weller. The Six-gun Samurai concentrated on its sound until he felt control of his body return. He opened his eyes and raised himself on one elbow.

"He's come to, Sheriff," a voice called from behind Tom's head.

Harvey Weller strode to where Tom lay on a bunk in the jail. "We did it, young feller. We sure enough did it. By damn, we got them crazies of Ashton's running and we didn't stop chasin' 'em until they was across the county line. Thanks to you, we were able to fight 'em off with only a couple bein' killed and a handfull bad hurt. Thought we were gonna lose you, though. That would have been a real shame, 'cause . . . we . . . we owe you a lot, Mr. Fletcher."

Tom managed, with a little help, to sit upright. "How are the Miller girls? Has anyone checked on them?" Blank looks swept around the room, as though to ask; what about them? Then stumbling, uncertain footsteps sounded on the boardwalk outside.

George Jones, the baker, entered with tears streaming down his face. In his arms he held the limp, lifeless body of Bobby Tucker. His haunted, raining eyes searched the room until they focused on Tanaka Tom. Anger flared then, mixing with grief and changing Jones's face into a mask of hatred.

"This is your fault, damn you, Fletcher! I told you not to let these children be a part of it. But, no, you wouldn't listen. *You might as well have killed Bobby yourself!*"

Murmurs rose in the room until the sheriff, his face gone pale, spoke first. "What happened?"

George Jones laid the boy on a cot in a cell opposite Tom. "H-he must have caught a slug near the end of it

142

all. There was so much noise, the fires, an' then us high-tailin' it out after Ashton's mob, nobody heard him call for help. Poor little feller must have leaked to death, it' weren't no big wound or anything. If . . . if he'd only had someone there." Jones suddenly whirled, directing his anger again on Tom Fletcher. "You caused this and you're gonna pay for it! Bobby was like . . . like a son to me. I've been . . . courtin' the Widow Tucker." Renewed anger flushed George's face red. "Then you come along and ruin it all, Mister. You pick the time and place and I'm gonna gun you down."

"George, George, take it easy." Sheriff Waller put an arm around the grief-maddened man's shoulder. "Don't make things worse than they are. You're no gunfighter."

"I can use a gun well enough to take on a sissy who uses a sword."

Tanaka Tom's reaction to the death of the boy he'd let get in the fight had been dictated by his samurai training. It is inevitable that men will fight battles. If one dies in his first, that is his *karma*. At least, he thought, little Bobby would be reborn a samurai for his honorable death in combat. The challenge George Jones hurled at him caused his temper to flare. Such insults demanded an immediate and deadly answer, yet he restrained himself. He realized that every man in the room had been deeply affected by the death of little Bobby, that he was the one out of custom here. He knew, too, that his antagonist was not an over-proud, drunkenly strutting minor samurai or boorish lout of a peasant daring the powers of the mighty to gain personal face. No, George Jones did not truly deserve the *iaijutsu* lightning draw, a *miri-uchi* right-strike slash opening his belly and spilling his guts on the ground. Nor would he receive the swift death of *yokomen*—side head stroke—decapitation. In a strange land, one must practice the strange, new ways of that people. He would not kill, he would instruct.

"Mr. Jones. I, too, am most sorry for Bobby's death. And I have even greater sorrow for his widowed mother. We can only accept that it was his *karma* to die in his first battle. Our belief that his soul will fly to Japan and be reborn as a warrior is of little consolation to you people of the Western world, but it is all I have to offer. One thing, though, must be made clear between us.

"This sword, of which you speak so lightly, is more than three hundred years old. No one knows how much blood it has spilled. Since it was given to me, at the age of fourteen, it has killed more than forty men. All of them were armed. Some of them had guns. Several attacked me two or more at a time. I do not wish to fight you. It would not be fair . . . to you."

Jones let heavy lids droop over his wide, incredulous eyes, once, twice, slowly a third time. "Uh . . . I reckon you don't pack that six-gun for show, then, either?"

"I do well enough with it, although I have not yet spent ten years perfecting its art, as I did with the *katana*. There will be peace between us, Mr. Jones?" Tom pressed the point.

George nodded, licked dry lips. He turned and walked out of the cell area, into the Sheriff's office. "I'd better go give . . . Bridget the bad nwes."

When the baker left the room, Tom pushed himself to his feet. A crushing headache blasted inside his head, causing the room to sway and he reached out to steady himself. "If that is settled then, and no one has news regarding the Miller girls, I shall go find out for myself."

"Not now, you won't," the doctor declared firmly, bustling over to press a pallid hand against the Six-gun Samurai's chest. "You're in no shape to go anywhere."

"I can manage. It is important to see the Miller girls are safe. The responsibility is mine." Tanaka Tom took a tottering step away from the bunk, then another. Dizziness rippled over him like the icy pounding of the Inland Sea. He paused in the cell entrance a moment, then walked on, each step growing stronger. Without

144

another pause or backward look, he made it to the outer door.

Tom's Morgan stallion had been rounded up and slip-reined to the tie-rail. Thankful for this in his present condition, he pulled himself into the saddle and turned the animal's head to the left. Back stiffened with samurai pride, he rode to the boardinghouse.

"Are the Miller girls all right?" Tom asked when Maw Tamblin answered his knock.

A pudgy hand flew to the gray-haired woman's mouth. "Why, mercy sakes, I don't know. You mean . . . all that excitement, the shootin' up town ain't over?"

"No. Ashton's been run off. You needn't stand guard down here any more. Let's go to their room and find out how they are."

The broken window, overturned commode with a spreading wet spot around the shattered water pitcher gave clear testimony to what had happened. Tanaka Tom spent little time looking for other answers. The pounding in his head, weakness in his limbs and body and compelling surge of nausea that cramped his stomach spoke louder than all the clamoring voices at the sheriff's office. He didn't have to like it, but he regretfully admitted that he would have to rest and recover.

He would delay his departure for New Caanaland until morning.

Chapter Eighteen

Bradley Ashton raged and fumed inwardly on the long ride back to Yellow Creek Valley. New Caanaland, his dream-come-true, threatened by a mob of fat-gut shopkeepers and saloon bums. How could that be? Total, humiliating defeat had been prevented only by Larry Don Saggerty's brilliant capture of the Miller girls.

No one, from what his chief gunslinger had told him, even knew they had invaded the boardinghouse and spirited the girls out a window. He'd have his revenge on them all the same, and so would Margaret. It would serve as an object lesson to the other sheep as well. Snow began some time during the night, making their retreat even more arduous, so that by the time they reached the last half mile to the village of New Caanaland, Ashton's aching body swayed with mind-numbing fatigue, making it nearly impossible to stay in the saddle. A cowled figure rode up beside him and, with a start, Ashton realized it was Margaret Dorn.

She threw back the hood of her heavy woolen garment, revealing a face alight with evil glee, lips drawn back in a grimace of triumph, eyes ablaze with madness. "I got me one. A snot-nosed brat about my brother's age. He was hidin' behind a pile of mattresses on the balcony of the hotel. I saw him from the alley and shot him in the side. He was bleedin' like a stuck hog when I left."

A strangled cackle of laughter broke from deep in Margaret's throat. She flung her head around, to look at Rachel and Martha Miller, who rode behind amid a cluster of guardian deacons. "Oh, you're gonna get yours, both of you. You're gonna burn, you hear me, burn!" Again the unnatural chortling bubbled out.

"What do you mean coming along like this? You could have been killed." Ashton's scolding words brought Margaret back to a semblance of reason.

"I . . . I had to make sure . . . a-about them. That they were captured or killed. Vengeance. Don't you see? The Almighty must have His vengeance and so must I." Noting Ashton's look of concern, she went on hurriedly. "That Brother Thomas. The one who escaped. I saw him there, in Aspen Gap. He was leading the fight against us. One of our men shot him down right after I killed the black-haired boy. Even he was made to pay."

"Praise be for that!" Ashton's mood changed, a frown of concern creasing his brow. "You're distraught, Margaret. We both need rest. We will talk more of it later, after some sleep and a meal. There's still the trial for these two and Helen Blair."

Margaret's lips curled in a cruel, expectant smile. "The trial. Yes, the trial!"

Before the first pale line of blue and rose backlighted the eastern crags, Tanaka Tom rode out of Aspen Gap in pursuit of Bradley Ashton. The time had come to finish what he'd come for. He had no idea where he would find Edward Hollister or others of his men. Perhaps in Denver. Tom had only a rumor that the evil colonel had gone there in the first place. It could be that Hollister had passed on through while each day the trail grew colder. Meanwhile he had to deal with Ashton . . . swiftly and permanently.

The man had gone insane. Tom had no doubt of that. Not the gray nether-world feeble-mindedness that afflicted some among the long-lived Japanese, but the berserk frenzy that sometimes came upon a samurai too long drenched in blood or *saki*. For a while Tom had thought he might find Bradley Ashton living a life of meditation and prayer, seeking to atone for his past evils. Had it been the case, Tom might have left him to his own way to Nirvana. Far to the contrary, though, Ashton's mad scheme to enrich himself over the grinding degradation of honest but simple-minded people clearly showed he had not changed from his days of rapine and murder along the Savannah River. Before Ashton died, though, Tom wanted the man to know the reason why.

He wanted to send Ashton screaming into the blackness of the underworld fully aware that the sins he committed against the Fletcher family would accompany him for eternity. He would not die as a samurai, to be reborn a warrior once more. No, Tom would make Ashton's death degrading and unclean so that his soul would forever roam in darkness. With this in mind, Tom brought along his pack mule, loaded with all his possessions. He would not be going back to Aspen Gap. Nothing remained there for him and the law might not take kindly to his plans. For Martha and their brief romance, he had equally short, brutally realistic thoughts. They had sensed a need in each other and had acted to fulfill it. They had found mutual satisfaction in the doing. But his mission came first. He must move on and had to do it alone. Once freed from Ashton's clutches and reunited with her father, Tanaka Tom felt confident, Martha would soon forget him, find a suitable man and settle down. With these many things in mind, Tanaka Tom pushed on toward his meeting with Ashton and the clash of their *karmas*.

The going wasn't easy, though. The previous night's snow had piled a new layer, unmelting under a lowering, slated sky. Noon came and passed, with Tom's animals plowing through chest-high drifts, before he reached the turn-off point and left the trail to work cross-country through the range of hills separating him from New Caanaland.

By four-fifteen that afternoon, Tanaka Tom had cautiously wormed his way to an observation point some six hundred yards above the roofs of New Caanaland.

148

He tied his horse and mule, brought along an extra blanket to sit upon and took up a patient watching of what went on below. The view proved interesting if not informative.

Groups of women, heavily clothed against the chill of onsetting evening and the still present snow, gathered sticks and branches. Walking among the outlying trees, they picked up windfalls and cut greener limbs, bundling them in sheaves approximately two hand-spans in thickness. Unusual for the gloom-filled community, they were singing. Tom heard their voices drifting up to him, reminding him of his childhood.

"Bringing in the sheaves, bringing in the sheaves. We shall come rejoicing, bringing in the sheaves."

Other activity caught his eye. A group of men in the central square were working with a corkscrew shaped auger, digging what looked like fencepost holes. First they shoveled away the trampled snow, then a man with a pick broke through the frost-rimmed crust. Next, two men, straddling the opening, began to wind the contrivance into the earth, giving it six complete turns, hefting it from the hole to dump its burden of soil, then returning it to place, working until the handle barely protruded. They continued the process until three holes had been completed. While they labored, Tom heard the distant ringing of axes and shifted his attention that way.

A dozen men came from the woods on the far side of the community, hefting on their shoulders three sturdy poles, each having a base diameter of some six inches. These they brought to the square in front of the church. There they hoisted them into the newly dug holes and dirt was firmly pounded in to make them stand upright. That task finished, the blacksmith and his helper approached.

They carried the ever present hammers and lengths of chain with crude shackles attached to each. Using large, hand-forged staple nails, they fastened a section of links to each post, tested their holding strength and departed. Tanaka Tom had a growing assurance he

149

knew what Ashton planned for these poles and decided he must attack soon after darkness fell.

A broad smile split the grim features of Travis McNee when he spotted the floundering marks of two animals leaving the main trail out of Aspen Gap. One ridden, one led. It had to be Fletcher. He'd get that bastard this time, get him good. God, what a horrible way to die, he thought, reflecting on the bloody, mutilated corpse of his partner, Clive Niebocker. He'd discovered the body when he awakened from his stupor two mornings ago, a large, painful knot behind one ear and his prisoner long gone. He'd never found his horse and had nothing to use to bury Clive. The coyotes and wolves would be feasting on the little bounty man now, Trav knew. No help for it though. He'd walked nearly ten miles before finding an isolated ranch house and acquiring a fresh mount. He wasted a day making wide casts until he located Tom's escape trail. He'd spent yesterday tracking the wanted man to the edge of Aspen Gap. He held up for the night, hearing sounds of a battle, then rode into Aspen Gap that morning.

Fletcher had left. He learned that within seconds of reaching the main street of the embattled community. Suspicious glances came his way and the sheriff questioned him for long, precious minutes while his quarry widened his lead. He felt a certain amazement that the girl, Martha Miller, had kept her word and not told the lawman about the treatment he and Clive had given her. She had pledged not to reveal them in return for their promise—which neither he nor Clive intended to keep—to bring Tom in alive for trial. In the end, even the poster from San Francisco failed to convince the men gathered at the jail that Fletcher, the man who had just saved their lives, could be a wanted criminal. The sheriff gave him a false lead, saying Fletcher headed east, toward Denver.

It took Trav an hour and a half to discover the ruse. He doubled back and forged out on this road until he made positive identification. The arrowhead flaw in one shoe print made it certain. How Clive would have loved to be in on the kill, he thought. Oh, well, a thousand dollars was a lot of money and it would go even farther if it didn't have to be divided two ways. Maybe he could even send for his wife and kids.

Oh, how he missed that woman. His boys, too. Why, they ought to be half-growed by now. He could show them the ropes around San Francisco. Maybe one would take to the bounty game with him. An' them cold, foggy nights with a fire in the potbelly stove and a warm woman who was his and his alone all snuggled up against him. Yeah. Might be he could afford to take a long spell off the trail after this one. Enjoy some of life while he could. First, though, he'd track down Fletcher and settle his hash. Strange how Fletcher seemed almost not to be human.

He'd torn through some mighty rough people in San Francisco. Taking on the Tong and Jeffrey Nash's bully boys. A lot of people died. Some that said Fletcher had killed Nash, too, as well as O'Neil. That's what the warrant was about. After seein' first-hand what Fletcher had done to the Larcher gang, McNee firmly resolved to take more care this time. To see he had every advantage and then swoop in, blast Fletcher into Hell and gone and go collect. That's the way he'd do it.

Darkness came early, a few fine flakes of new snow drifted down on the brim of Tanaka Tom's hat as he sat munching cold jerky and a handful of parched corn, waiting for the cold of night and boredom to dull the senses of any sentries and make his entry into New Caanaland easier. He would locate the girls and sneak them out as smoothly as Ashton's men had accomplished it at Maw Tamblin's. By daylight they would be far away, taking Pete Miller with them. Ashton would be dead and no pursuit could be expected from the people of the valley, once freed from the bondage of their dosages of peyote. As to the gunslingers, they worked for pay. With the man who controlled the purse strings dead, they wouldn't ride after Tom for free. It should be simple.

He'd get Ashton first, then the girls.

Chapter Nineteen

A thick, lowering overcast gave an almost tangible quality to the darkness. Tanaka Tom Fletcher, dressed in dark clothing and armed with only his *katana* and six-gun, skirted the village of New Caanaland, choosing to enter from the direction of the peyote field. His last observations before night fell indicated everything to be as before. He soon found that to be in error.

"Hey, Latigo! You hear that?"

"Hear what?"

"I thought I heard somebody slippin' around in the trees out there."

"Imagination."

"Naw. I mean it, Latigo."

"Well, you figger there's something to it, you gotta look for yourself. We both can't leave here. Larry Don'd give us hell if he caught the two of us out there."

"Sure, Latigo, I'll do it."

Tanaka Tom crouched low, remaining motionless while the guard thrashed around in the underbrush, finding nothing. Men on watch this far from the settlement? He'd not seen them here before. Ashton must have sent them out after dark, Tom thought. He'd have to use even more caution in moving. He remained where he'd knelt for several minutes after the empty-handed deacon returned to his post.

Swiftly Tom rose and moved back into the woods some twenty yards. He made a complete circle of the area, noting that the new guards had been placed in such a manner that not even a rabbit's movement toward the village would go unnoticed. Ashton was taking no chances. Yet, Tom decided, his original plan of entry seemed best.

Taking careful, though swift, strides, Tom soon reached a point near the peyote field, his mind still filled with unanswered questions. Did anyone check on these guards? If so, how often? He had little time to wait to see the answer for himself. He wanted to finish his business with Ashton, free the Miller girls and be well on his way long before daylight. There were not two men at each post. His quick circuit had showed him that. He'd have to gamble. The light, nearly constant breeze that blew through the valley stiffened as yet another storm front approached. Tom felt it on his cheek, then heard it rustling through a field of ripening corn off a ways to his left. Nature, as his samurai training had taught him, can often be bent to the warrior's use. The time had come to make his move.

Tom crouched low to the grounnd and thought of himself as a rock, an old samurai trick for mental control of the body. He headed toward the cornfield, angled out of his place in the trees to cross a narrow strip of cleared ground. He paused often, held his breath until once again on the move. His cautious approach consumed a full ten minutes to cross fifteen yards. With great relief he slid among the cornstalks, his presence adding little to the constant sibilant clatter. The sere, brown leaves, yellowed stalks, and drying ears concealed both sight and sound of his passage. In less than three minutes, Tanaka Tom hunkered down behind a low stone fence that marked the village end of the field.

His eyes, well accustomed to the dark, carefully searched for an inner line of sentries, confident he would find them easily. A minute passed, then another. Two men approached from opposite directions, stopped to exchange a few words a scant twenty feet from where Tanaka Tom knelt. One guard rolled a cigarette, struck a lucifer with his thumbnail and touched fire to his smoke.

"Sure would like to be in that meetin'," the man said through smoke curling from his mouth and nostrils.

"What for? You don't think you'd get to see any tender young skin, do you? The boss saves all that for hisself, except for the worn out ones he tosses to us and that Margaret. Man, can she screw."

"Margaret? You're kiddin' me."

"I'll allow she don't do it no more, now she's gotten so high and mighty. But back a couple of years ago she'd come down to the bunkhouse right regular, ever' time ol' Ashton was outta the valley. Work her way through the whole crew in one night. Never seemed to get enough. But those days are gone forever." He sighed heavily. "Well, we'd best be headin' back the other way. Don't forget to douse that smoke before you run into any of that holier-than-thou bunch. They'd go screamin' to Ashton about it."

The smoker snorted derisively. "Right you are. They're all a bunch of crazies, you ask me."

"Including the boss?"

"Especially the boss. Keep your eyes open."

"Sure enough."

When the men's backs disappeared into the darkness, Tanaka Tom vaulted the fence and made a dash in among the nearest buildings. He'd make his way first to the parsonage and check on Ashton. His lips curled downward as he contemplated the way he would tell Ashton the reason he must die. He dare not take pleasure in it, Tom reprimanded himself. Ashton represented but one less name on the list, which meant that all the sooner he could go after Edward Hollister. Grimly he started toward the small house beside the church.

Flaming torches, flickering wildly in the stout wind, brightly lighted the main square. Every window of the church blazed with light from kerosene lanterns inside. In contrast, the parsonage sat dark and squat, giving an abandoned appearance. Tanaka Tom waited patiently in a narrow passage between two buildings. He watched for a while, making sure no one had the area under

155

observation. Satisfied, he dashed quickly from shadow to shadow to the distant side of Ashton's residence.

A brief check convinced Tom that no one lurked around the building. He entered through the back door and went quietly from room to room. Except for the servant, Joe, sleeping in his pantry room, the place was empty. Ashton and his guards had left. The center of attraction had to be the church, Tom decided. He let himself out the way he'd entered and carefully worked his way to a spot in deep shadow under an open window in the nave.

"Hear the judgment of the Almighty," Bradley Ashton intoned to the tightly packed congregation inside the church. " 'Thou shalt not suffer a witch to live.' The injunction is quite clear, beloved Brothers and Sisters. Is is not?"

"Amen! Amen!" cried the stuporous followers of the mad cleric.

"Here, then, the testimony of our beloved Elder Sister."

Margaret Dorn took Ashton's place in the pulpit, raising both hands over her head in a gesture taught her by Ashton. "On many occasions over the past year I have, late at night, come upon that one . . ." the index finger of her right hand lashed downward, condemningly pointing out Martha Miller. Ooohs and mumbles of displeasure rose in the audience. After a dramatic pause, Margaret went on.

"Yes, Martha Miller. I found her engaged in unnatural practices with her own sister, Rachel, and Helen Blair. Most recently, not three weeks ago, during the full moon, I came upon them in a forest glen. The two younger girls, fully unclothed, knelt before Martha, who wore but a white cord knotted about her hips. Martha spoke in an unearthly voice, words mumbled in a language not known to man. All the while her arms and fingers writhed over the bowed heads of these children, making mystical passes, while she called on them to give up their souls to Lucifer.

156

"And the girls cried out, their bodies trembling, 'Hail Satan, my Lord and my Master!' Sickened and frightened I . . . I failed in my faith and ran from the place."

Cries of anger, shouts of dismay and a low rumble of hate filled the small wooden structure. Outside, the Six-gun Samurai felt a coldness walk his spine and believed himself to be in the presence of some ancient and unspeakably malignant *mikoto*—the spirits from before the beginning of man. From inside, he heard Margaret's voice, filled with venom, go on concocting her fanciful tale of horror.

"Then, the night before two of these wicked girls fled from redemption, I spied upon them, all three, dancing naked in a fairy ring in the same clearing, weaving a spell to protect Rachel from the power of our Divine Father, the Reverend Master.

"Oh, yes, they knew long before we did. The Devil came to them and told them that Rachel was to be chosen for the Sacred Sisterhood. Being witches they could not allow this. But their power was not strong enough and they ran away. Only Helen could not escape. When she was summoned to the service of the Reverend Master, she decided to act.

"When the time was right, she attacked us with a knife. She severely cut our beloved Reverend Master and stabbed me. Here, see for yourselves." Margaret jerked open her white robe, and exposed the jagged red lips of her wound. "Later Helen confessed to her practice of witchcraft."

"No! It's not true, none of it!" Helen shrieked. She leaped from her chair, small hands pressed over her ears, as though to ban Margaret's condemning lies from her hearing. "I'm not a witch. None of us are. We aren't! It . . . it . . . none of it happened like Margaret said. She's the one. She came to me in the night. She made me do awful, dirty things with her and then took me to the Reverend Master. Th-they both took off their clothes and wanted me to do t-those t-t-things a-again."

"Enough!" Ashton thundered a bit too late, making a sign to two deacons to silence Helen. "Hear, Brothers and Sisters, hear how Satan has seized her tongue and made her say these frightful things? Is anyone more pure and saintly that our dear Elder Sister, Margaret Dorn? What a false and evil accusation this wicked little girl has made! What do you say, beloved people of New Canaaland? What is to be done with them?"

"*Death,*" Margaret prompted in a barely audible hiss.

"The witches must die," a farmer in the front row declared in a rumbling, room-filling bass.

"To the stake!" several women in the choir box chanted.

"Burn them! Death to all witches!"

"Take them then and let justice be done according to the will of the Almightly. To the blacksmithy's shop with them. There shackle them to the roof posts and let them await the dawn and their punishment." Ashton stood on the edge of the altar platform urging on the congregation. Rough hands seized the three sobbing, terrified girls and dragged them outside.

The Six-gun Samurai had barely time enough to slide into the darkness and avoid detection.

Tanaka Tom Fletcher found he had to make a conscious effort to shake the impression of malevolence; to replace the fanciful bad *mikoto* from that time before the *kami* came with good for man, with the unsettlingly real evil of the deranged Ashton and his equally vile companion, Margaret. Did no one else hear the inconsistencies and the false note of her twisted logic? First she was supposed to have last seen them some three weeks ago, then she again spies on the girls on the night before the Miller girls fled from New Caanaland. Had the scene she described been true, with Martha and the others speaking in a tongue unknown to humans, how then could she, Margaret, know what it was they said?

But religious excess sometimes blinded and deafened a man to all except what he wished to hear and see.

How much more so for a mob besotted by the powerful spirit of the peyote plant? Thinking these dark thoughts, Tom cautiously worked his way to the blacksmith shop, trying to devise a means of freeing the girls. He could not allow Ashton's plans to come to fruition.

Rachel he knew to be a child of sweet and innocent disposition. Martha, whose passion and the delights of her mature, though youthful, body he held in great fondness, was likewise innocent of the incredible things ascribed to them by Margaret Dorn. He could think no less of Helen, although he knew nothing of her past or how she had come to be accused with the others. Even at the risk of having to come back for Ashton, he had to get them away from here first. Outside the smithy he paused at the sound of voices.

"That ought to hold them, Latigo."

"Sure enough. Hey, think we could . . . uh, you know . . . hee-hee-hee. Nobody'd know or care much what with them gettin' roasted in the morning."

"Hummm. You got a thought there, Latigo. Even if it came outta that outhouse mind of yourn. We'd better wait, though, until everybody's quited down a bit. Uh! Ah . . . Good evenin', Elder Sister. Come to see to their spiritual comfort?"

Margaret Dorn smiled bleakly, her voice icily formal. "Yes. Something like that, Deacon Fisher. Leave us alone now. They can't harm me."

"If you say so. We'll be back later. An' some of the boys is only a shout away."

"Thank you." Margaret sighed heavily and paced the floor until the men walked out of earshot. Then she rounded on the helpless girls. "You see where your defiance has gotten you? You," she shook a finger in Helen's face. "You tried to raise your power against mine. A lot of good it did you. Why do you think I suggested that exotic little scene to dear Bradley? I knew you had no stomach for it. Oh, so very fancy and ladylike, the lot of you. Too good for this, too nice for that, too pure to let Brad touch your saintly body." She savagely pinched the sobbing Rachel's cheek. "You'll learn, all

159

of you. You'll learn tomorrow morning what it means to defy the Reverend Master and . . . and to defy me!"

"You're a horrid person, Margaret Dorn," Helen spat defiantly. "An awful, evil, rotten person."

"Your words mean nothing to me. Tomorrow you will all be dead, burned at the stake and I'll still be here."

Helen's momentary strength dissolved and she slumped with her head in her lap, sobbing. Rachel also began to cry bitterly. Martha's eyes blazed with fury.

"I know someone who can stop you. He's the one who saved Aspen Gap and drove you all away."

"Do you mean that man with the ridiculous sword?" At Martha's nod, Margaret released a bark of laughter. "He's no good to you any more. He stopped a bullet in the street outside the sheriff's office not long after Larry Don grabbed you and your sister. His body's feedin' the worms by now."

All hope fled Martha and with a shriek of despair she fell into a sobbing, defeated heap. A shrill peal of mad laughter came from Margaret's mouth and she left the blacksmith shop, headed for the parsonage and Brad Ashton's bed.

Cautiously Tanaka Tom Fletcher slid away from the side of the blacksmithy, blending into the shadows. His mind carefully mulled over the difficulties facing him. Guards inside and out where the girls were being held. Not mind-dulled members of Ashton's congregation, but clearheaded gunslingers, poised for action. More sentries walking the streets of the village, at its outer edge and beyond near the screening trees in the distance. It seemed impossible to penetrate this envelope of security and get the Miller girls and Helen Blair out of there, so why not let them be brought to him?

Yes. In the morning, with everyone in the open, all attention turned to the ritual murder of the girls, that would be the time to strike. He would need a diversion. That could be worked out later. If he could time it right, attack before the girls were chained to the execution posts, he might be able to kill Ashton and end it all there. It would work better if he had an ally inside the village, someone who could trigger the diversion or at least take arms from a fallen gunman and join the battle. Sudden realization came that he had such a man. The father of two of the victims, Pete Miller, would be willing to help. Tom hurried in the direction of the Miller cottage.

"Who is it?" a tense, strained voice inquired in whispered answer to Tanaka Tom's knock.

"Brother Thomas. The man who said he might call on you for help at some time."

The bar rattled and slid away. Pete Miller opened the door a crack, wide enough to allow his visitor to enter. Inside Tom saw two other men near the table. One held a butcher knife, the other hefted a hand axe.

"If you can throw that properly," the Six-gun Samurai observed to the hatchet man, "it can be as effective as a six-gun. Silent, too." Tom recalled his recent fight in San Francisco against the Blue Dragon Tong who favored, and were highly efficient with, the short handled *Fu* hatchet.

Pete Miller made the introductions, indicated a chair drawn up at the hand-made table. When Tom moved toward it, Pete revealed himself further.

"I figured you were up to somethin', that I might be seein' you again."

"How's that?"

"I saw you not take your communion buttons. I . . . I'd figured that out myself and hadn't taken any for near a month. Same for Brice and Art here. We've wanted to . . . do something about Ashton. We had no idea how or what, but now we have no choice. We might not get away with it, I don't know. I only know that I will not see my daughters die the horrible death Ashton has planned for them. I'll be dead or they will before he can do it."

Tanaka Tom peered intently into the earnest faces around him, then nodded with satisfaction. "I think,

161

Miller-*san*, that together we may be able to end Ashton's reign of madness and free your daughters alive at the same time. I have a plan, if you will listen to it."

Half an hour later, after discussion and modification of Tanaka Tom's basic plan, the meeting broke up. The Six-gun Samurai slipped through the sleeping streets of New Caanaland toward the church to prepare a most unpleasant surprise for Bradley Ashton.

Chapter Twenty

Tanaka Tom Fletcher carefully extinguished the small fire over which he had cooked a portion of rice and brewed strong, green tea. He used a large clump of dirt, covered with a thick layer of snow. Tom turned it upside down and dumped it on the coals, stamping it solidly in place so that no betraying coil of smoke rose into the pale blue sky of early morning. Next, he began his most important task.

From the large parfleche bags of his packsaddle, Tanaka Tom took the various parts of his armor and laid them out on the rocks surrounding his campsite. Then he removed his clothing and took a cleansing bath in stingingly cold handsfull of snow. Custom satisfied, he dressed in a new, clean white silk loincloth. Next he donned the lightly padded *shatsu* and *kame,* the undershirt and knee-length trousers that served the same purpose of a medieval knight's jupon. Although he seemed unaware of it, time passed rapidly while he worked at a seemingly casual rate, so far only a third of the way garbed for battle. Tom continued his ritual with the inexorable slowness of a matador's dressing ceremony.

First Tom lifted the *kusazuri* and swung its bulk around his waist. It was made of twisted and braided rice stems, backed by the *yazuri no gawa,* the "protection-from-arrows skirt" of fire-hardened bone over pliable leather. He made a double wrap of the *koshi no o* hip strap and tied it securely so that the skirted *kusazuri* formed a split-front protection for his thighs.

Next, he poked his head through the oval opening of the hinged chest and back pieces of the *tsuru bashiri* corselet of lacquered, fire-hardened wood inlaid with strips of bone and horn. He made sure the built-in shoulder pads lay properly, then tightened the thong, tying it so that ample play remained in the *tsubo no ita*, vertical strips of hardwood woven into an accordian-pleat of seagrass cloth which allowed ventilation and freedom of movement while still protecting the wearer's sides. Before he went further, Tom knelt and attached the *ashi no mamoru* greaves below his knees.

Next he stood and drew on the long, gauntletlike arm pieces of the *sode no tebukuro*, then draped the heavy *sode* over his shoulders. The four-layered mantle—*sendan no ita, kyubi no ita, munu-ita,* and *kamakuri-ita*—made respectively of lacquered hardwood covered with seawater hardened leather, bone, brass, and horn, formed sleeves protecting shoulders and upper arms. The entire affair was held in place by the stout cord of the *shoji no ita*, from which hung loose breastplates of the same material as the *sode*, all of which was decorated with braided, lacquered rice straw in the same design as the *kusazuri*. He settled and tied each piece in place carefully, then swung into position the crested *shikoro* that covered shoulders and neck. From the rock where his helmet rested, Tom took a mask.

Similar to those worn by actors in the ancient Greek theater, the carved wooden face was done in a grotesque grimace of fury, eyes squinted, lips drawn back in a snarl, mouth open. It had been painted to lifelike reality, except for tinges of green; and a few wisps of human hair swayed down from the upper lip forming a scaggly warrior's moustache. Next Tanaka Tom slipped his *tabi* clad feet into hardwood sandals with *tatami* matting platforms, their thongs protected from being cut by studs of brass and bone. He wound a wide *koshi-obi* girdle around his middle and inserted his two swords. All that remained was to don his helmet.

Tanaka Tom had always preferred an Oshi Eboshi-type helmet worn by the Maeda of Kaga Province. On his seventeenth birthday, when he was promoted in the *rentai* to the rank of *sho-i-tai*—roughly equivalent to a freshly turned out second lieutenant in the army—his adopted father, Tanaka Nobunara, presented him with a priceless one from the middle Edo period, made about 1725. The helm itself was constructed of fire-hardened hardwood, grooved and inlaid with strips of brass with the entire outer surface done in hundreds of coats of black lacquer. The inner facings were done in gold and red lacquer. The *fukigaeshi*, or protective wings, sweeping to the sides from behind the *mae-bashi*—visor—were intricately carved and inlaid with gold. The *shikoro*—neck protector—was made of overlapping plates of curved hardwood in the manner of the *sendan no ita* of the *sode*, tied in place with stout seagrass cords, lacquered black and studded with lumps of gold and precious stones. Tom had chosen to bring this one with him on his quest in America.

He lifted the priceless helmet and placed it firmly and comfortably on his head. He crossed the thick, leather-covered cords of seagrass under his chin and wound the loose ends twice about his neck, tying them in back and tucking the tails under the back plate of his armor. In only a few minutes he would be on his way to New Caanaland.

Travis McNee jerked short on the reins, causing his horse to set its front feet, joints locked, while its tender mouth and tongue worked in painful protest to the cruel cutting of the bit. McNee's face twisted into a tortured grimace, an expression that served him as a smile. The tracks in the melting snow at his feet were fresh, no older than the previous night. He had his quarry cornered now. Caught between his gun and the religious crazies down in the valley, Fletcher could not escape him now. McNee ground-reined his mount and worked his way to the top of the low rise.

Looking below, some seven hundred yards away, he saw the man he hunted standing naked in the snow, rubbing himself with great handfulls of the frigid stuff, seeming to enjoy it as much as a hot shower from a sun-warmed barrel of fresh spring water. Taking great care McNee floundered through the drifts, hidden from Tom by trees, until he had narrowed the distance to some five hundred yards.

McNee steadied his rifle on his shoulder and took aim. He controlled his breathing and began taking up slack in the trigger. A downhill shot again. Not the best of all possible conditions. He remembered his previous bad luck at long range and reluctantly lowered his piece. He'd have to get closer, he grudgingly decided. McNee moved stealthily through the trees and under-brush, watching his target dress. He stopped abruptly, his mouth dropping open, when Tom picked up his *kusazuri*. What in hell, he wondered, is that weird tucker he's puttin' on? McNee stayed crouched behind a snow-covered boulder while Tom fitted into the *sode no tebukuro, sode and shikoro*. God, it looked like the fool was makin' up for a costume party. Once he'd overcome his consternation, Travis McNee started forward again.

Only a few feet separated the two men now. McNee couldn't believe that Fletcher hadn't heard him moving through the snow, but the wanted man had now turned his back and picked up something, fiddling with a tie string behind his head. Tanaka Tom faced around once more an Trav had to stifle a gasp at sight of the fright-mask. Fletcher pivoted away, reaching for his helmet and McNee decided the time had come to end it.

Slowly he stepped from behind the cover of a huge pine tree and raised his rifle to his shoulder. McNee took careful aim at the center of Tom's back. As he squeezed the slack out of the trigger, the man he'd come to kill suddenly whirled, his hand dipped into the top of his *obi*.

Tom produced a *shuriken* as he dropped to one side and McNee's first bullet zipped through empty space, the heavy Sharps buffalo rifle booming dully in the muffled stillness of snow covered hills. With a flick of his wrist, the Six-gun Samurai sent the tiny death star whizzing through the air. Two bare steel points buried firey prongs in Trav McNee's stomach as he levered another round into the chamber.

Rather than triggering the rifle, reflexes responded to enormous agony and sent McNee's hands to his hurting belly. McNee looked up and, through pain-watered eyes, saw the hideous battle mask descend on him as Tanaka Tom closed in, *katana* raised in one hand.

Incense rose in sickeningly sweet tendrils from around the three execution stakes. It was an idea Ashton had obtained from reading about the burning of witches in Europe during the Inquisition. It helped prevent the spectators from becoming nauseous at the stench of charring human flesh. The Brahman caste in India did it also for their funeral pyres. In addition, he'd arranged for branches of wild sage and slabs of cedar bark to be worked into the fagots that would be piled around the girls. He considered his efforts ingenious, the effect created a pleasant, aromatic experience. From the belfry of the church, Ashton observed the people of New Caanaland assembling for the ritual he was about to enact.

Ashton felt his pulse quicken with anticipation as the congregation ended their shuffling and jostling for position, forming three sides of a hollow square with the stakes midway inside, the open-end toward the church doors. A smile of satisfaction split his face. They were calm and obedient, more docile than they had been for some time. That was his doing too.

He had decreed that a double portion of peyote be ingested at the evening vespers and that again this morning, four buds were to be eaten by every adult, two by the children. There would also be a communion service before the fires were lighted, sending those willful, disobedient girls off to their just reward. He forced himself to wait another long, dramatic minute, then descended the spiral staircase and assembled his retinue of deacons.

Gowned in his cowled robe of soft, golden cloth, Ashton presented an awsome sight standing in the open

167

portals of the church. He had a symbolic sword of retribution and ecclesiastical authority tightly belted around his waist. It had been his father's blade, a Knight's Templer Masonic ritual sword. Ashton raised his arms in benediction, one hand clutching a Bible. Behind him, a line of three deacons softly rang small bells. To their rear, feeling equally as foolish as the trio in front, four gunslinging deacons held large, fat candles, their guttering flames protected from the brisk morning breeze by paper cones.

How appropriate, Ashton thought. *Bell, book, and candle. The proper way to exorcise three witches.* He lowered his arms and, with stately tread, began the slow, solemn procession to the burning place. The entourage halted before the stakes. Again Ashton paused for dramatic effect.

"Bring forth the witches," he intoned in a loud and somber voice.

From the direction of the blacksmith shop came the sound of shrill feminine voices, raised in pitiful, frightened pleading. The spectators heard the meaty smack of a large, hard palm slapping a tender cheek and silence followed. Then a cluster of deacons appeared on the street, each pair holding between them the slumped, slack-legged form of one of the prisoners. They found it necessary to drag the condemned girls to their place of execution.

They had nearly reached the spot, the whole of the girls' vision filled with the ominous sight of the death stakes to which they would be tied, when Rachel and Helen began to sob and scream hysterically. The guards struggled with them, wrestling both children into place before the posts. Martha, on the other hand, gained control over her body, standing erect and shaking off the hands of the men who delivered her to her doom. Shoulders straight, back ramrod stiff, chin held proudly high, she walked the last few yards unassisted. Her grave expression heightened the effect of her haughty, queenly gait. When each girl stood at her stake, the posts between them and the demented preacher, facing Ashton, he began a sermon.

"Of all the sins, the blackest is disobedience of the Almighty. Running away from your parents and the authority of the church, lying to outsiders about the practices of our religion, blaspheming and denying your rightful place in our sacred community . . . all of these . . . yea, even witchcraft, are as nothing before your disobedience."

"You're a great one to talk about disobeying God, you lying degenerate!" Pete Miller, his face crimson with fury, yelled defiantly at Bradley Ashton. "So help me, you'll not kill these innocent girls!"

Two of the congregation standing near him grabbed the raging father of two of the victims, holding him while he struggled helplessly. Ashton saw they had the situation under control and spoke to them.

"Thank you, Brothers. Take him to the church and restrain him there until this is over. The man is distraught," Ashton explained to the congregation. "Under the circumstances that is understandable. The sins of the children shall not be inherited by the father. Let him go in peace and pray for his healing. Now, to return to the matter at hand . . ."

Tanaka Tom's *katana* sang through the air, striking sparks off the steel barrel of McNee's rifle, cleaving through the wooden forestock. Despite the wound he had suffered, this man had strength and lightning reflexes, Tom realized, stepping back and again raising his sword for a *shoman* overhand cut, used to slice a man open vertically from neck to crotch. When the blade descended, McNee swung his long gun like a quarter-staff, then screamed when he lost three fingers of his right hand. Without conscious thought, he leaped backward, to widen the distance between him and his attacker.

This fight would take longer than he expected, Tom thought. Longer than he wanted. "Who are you? Why do you attack me?"

McNee answered Tom's question with one of his own. "You are Thomas Fletcher?"

"I am."

"My name is Travis McNee. I have a warrant charging you with three murders and arson in San Francisco. You're wanted dead or alive."

"I murdered no one in San Francisco. I fought only to defend my life or that of others."

"That's not how the police look at it. One of the men you killed was one of theirs; Lieutenant O'Neil."

"That's not true. O'Neil was killed by a member of Madame Kuming's Tong, not I."

"No matter. I came to get you on a lawful warrant and I figger takin' in a dead man's less hassle than takin' one in alive." While they verbally fenced McNee bound up the severed stubs of his fingers to stop further loss of blood.

"You count your victories before they are won, McNee-*san*. It is you who shall die, not I." Tanaka Tom punctuated his last words with a charge, his blade held in the horizontal plane to his right side. He made a roundhouse swing that should have cut McNee in two.

Tanaka Tom's *katana* sliced through Travis McNee's heavy sheepskin coat but failed to score in flesh as the big bounty hunter jumped backward once more, reaching awkwardly with his left hand for the holstered Colt on his right hip.

Inside the vestibule of the church Peter Miller stood between the two men who had brought him there. Out of sight of the others now, he allowed himself a crinkled smile of satisfaction. So far everything had gone according to plan. To left and right, Brice Cantrell and Art Fellows returned the grin. Outside, Ashton could be heard winding up his sermon. It would happen any second now. They'd have to get busy.

"Pray, Brothers and Sisters. Pray. Beg the Almighty to forgive their sins and have mercy on these blighted souls. Pray for New Caanaland's never-ending power. Amen!" The deacons began passing out peyote buttons. "Take freely of the sacred bread of our communion with the Almighty. Take it and nourish your souls with spiritual food." Then he turned to those holding the victims.

"These women have been tried and found guilty of witchcraft. The Almighty demands that they be purified by the fire and the cross." He drew his sword and held its point high in the shimmering morning air. "Take them to the place of their suffering, bind them to the stakes with stout cords, and pile high about them fragrant boughs. Bring forth sacred fire from the High Holy Altar and let it enfold them that they might find redemption in its purging flames. Anathema! Anathema! Anathema! Satan be gone!"

Ashton felt a rush of elation. He'd gotten through that part of the ancient formula without a single mistake. He felt a surge of blood to his loins, stiffening him. Considering the gender of those about to die a young girl to satisfy his need seemed inappropriate. Why not Robbie? So energetic and inventive a lad for such tender years. Yes, he'd do. Brad Ashton made mental note to summon Robbie Williams to serve him that night as he walked with theatrical tread through the line of posts and turned to face the frightened girls.

Helen Blair's mind had mercifully retreated from the horror of what was happening. When she felt the hard, rough hands of the two deacons grab her shoulders, though, reality came frighteningly back to her. Shrieking hysterically, she lashed out with both arms, small hands closed into solid little fists. She hit one gunslinger in the mouth, splitting his lip, a trickle of blood running down to drip off his chin. They dragged her to the post all the same, lashed her tightly about the waist and shackled her hands, then began to pile tied fagots of dry wood around her until only her face showed above the gray-brown vastness. Tears splashed from her eyes and a raw, endless scream tore from her throat, her mouth twisted in agony as her body anticipated the flames soon to come.

"What the hell's gone wrong?" Pete Miller asked the

others, his mind frantically churning. He recognized his daughter, Rachel's, voice screaming and begging for mercy while Ashton's deacons and acolytes fastened her to the stake. "It's got to be now. But how can we three do it alone? How can we stop them?"

"He'll be here, don't worry," Brice assured Pete.

Pete's blank, stricken face turned to the other men, one damp, trembling hand holding a length of black fuse, the other a kitchen lucifer. "What if he doesn't come?"

Martha Miller's turn came last. The two deacons started forward with her, then halted abruptly when they heard a distant, shouted alarm.

Killing Travis McNee had taken a great deal more time and effort than Tanaka Tom had expected. The man fought with near maniacal strength, absorbing punishment and blood-letting wounds with the stoic determination of a true samurai. Tom's admiration grew as the struggle continued. At last McNee slipped on a patch of snow and he sprawled on the muddy, churned-up ground. Tom's *katana* flashed and McNee's head rolled in the mire. At least, Tom thought as he cleaned the blade and returned it to the scabbard, he shall return as a warrior. Perhaps in his new life he might find better *karma* and work at doing good. He quickly went to his Morgan stallion, strapped on his six-gun, fastened the plate armor skirt around the horse's chest and forelegs and tied it to his saddle. He mounted and rode swiftly down toward the valley.

Now as the Six-gun Samurai thundered down on the startled perimeter guard, the man rose, opened his mouth and shouted a warning cry. He made no second sound of alarm. Tanaka Tom's *katana* whistled through the air and the guard fell in two pieces, cut through the middle the undirected legs drumming out a death tattoo while the dying torso tried to crawl a few paces distance on rapidly weakening arms.

In an instant a swirl of dust covered the scene and Tom Fletcher rode on, closed in on the second rank of

172

sentries and blasted his way between a pair of them. The roaring Colt in his left hand scored a direct hit in one guard's right eye, the bullet bulging his head while whipping him off his feet a fraction of a second before his skull exploded outward in a shower of fragments and blood. Again without hesitation, Tanaka Tom bore down on the assembled congregation around the execution site.

Those same people, their minds fogged with peyote, looked up at the apparition descending on them and felt their beings filled with unspeakable horror. Almost as one their besotted brains recorded the hideous image of Tanaka Tom in his full battle armor, fright mask glaring wildly at them, his horse in the same black and gold array of armor, charging at them. Here was the Devil incarnate, their befuddled consciousness told them, come to rescue his servants in their hour of peril. All the hellfire and brimstone images conjured in endless sermons by Bradley Ashton welled up to haunt their conscious impressions, to bring shrieking, terrified flight in the wake.

In the same instant that the congregation dissolved into yelling, panic-stricken individuals, the fuse in the church sputtered to life and Pete Miller rushed out the door, followed by his two companions. They fell on the nearest deacons, driving them to the ground with flailing fists, disarming them and rushing to fire at others nearby. Tanaka Tom continued on toward the stakes, where a startled Latigo Crowell stood with a blazing torch in one hand, stopped in the act of applying it to Helen Blair's pyre.

The Six-gun Samurai's Colt blazed and the heavy 255-grain slug smashed into the gunslinging deacon's chest, driving him to the ground. Latigo's torch fell harmlessly a few feet away from the piled fagots. Bradley Ashton's tenuous hold on sanity seemed to snap in that moment and he turned, to scream maddened defiance at the demonic rider who pressed down on him.

Ashton raised his dulled, ceremonial sword, slashing wildly with it. Steel met steel and the superb Motohira

173

blade sliced through the softer metal of Ashton's espada like a hot knife through soft cheese. For an instant Ashton stared disbelievingly at the severed weapon, then threw it from him and ran for his life. Behind him, Tanaka Tom swerved aside and rode to the girls. There would be time for Ashton later, he could not escape.

Ignoring the fleeing, demoralized Ashton and his terrified flock, Tom used his *katana* and feet to knock away the stacked fagots. A few strokes with his blade and the soft iron of the hand-forged chain parted, freeing Helen. She nearly hampered Tom's movement as she fled to Rachel's stake and threw her arms around the wailing girl, pushing away the last of the brands as she did. Tom sliced through the soft, pigiron links of Rachel's bonds and turned to Martha. In the instant Tom swung to free Martha, he caught sight of movement from the corner of his eye.

A white-robed figure charged down on Tom, shrieking with demented fury, features hidden in the deep cowl. Tom's movement with his sword was hampered by his closeness to the burning stake and he had no time to change hands. His left arm dipped and his fingers closed around the cold steel links of his *kusarigama* chain. He jerked it free from the leather saddle bindings and began to whip it into a *sukuiuchi*—figure eight—pattern in the air.

Margaret Dorn felt an almost sexual delight watching the frightened girls being led to their doom. Moisture flowed from her innermost parts and ran stickily down her legs. Her heart beat faster as the deacons fastened each one in turn to the stakes and their terror overcame them. All except Martha Miller, damn her. Then the fire came forward and all would be well. Suddenly, without warning, she saw her joy wrestled from her grasp.

At the first shout of the unfortunate sentry, Margaret spun on one heel and looked at an apparition beyond her wildest and most disturbed dreams. A scale-covered demon directly from the pits of Hell raced down on the execution site, a shining sword in one hand. She stood, transfixed and unable to move, while the demonic creature thundered over all opposition, at last closing with Brad Ashton, who weakly tried to fend off the attack with his ceremonial blade. Shouting, screaming, terrified people raced by her on all sides, yet Margaret could not bring herself to make any sort of move. When Ashton lost his weapon and scrambled bleatingly away to safety, she saw her dreams of wealth and position crumbling with him. A shriek of pure fury rasped in her throat and burst from her lips. She grabbed up a dead guard's rifle and, ignoring her own danger, flung herself at the hateful rider who now paused in his swath of death to free the girls at the stake.

Tanaka Tom's *kusarigama* hummed and whistled through the air, lashing sideways and downward from the peak of its figure-eight so that the sickle tip bit deeply into white cloth and tender flesh beyond at the conclusion of the *shohatsu*—horizontal strike. With a snap of his wrist, Tanaka Tom brought it out, slicing through both of Margaret Dorn's carotid arteries and her larynx. She died without a sound, falling in a disordered, blood-soaked heap. Tom quickly cut Martha free and she rushed to the other girls. Satisfied, Tanaka Tom looked up to see Ashton fleeing toward the church. At the same moment, Tom's little diversion went off.

Five sticks of powder bulged the walls of the small church, sending flying shards of glass from the windows to cut indiscriminately at the innocent faithful and their tyrannical deacons alike. Women screamed and men shouted in angry pain. Then they saw the roaring blaze that ate into the dry wood of their house of worship. Fear and shock-driven adrenalin cleared the drug haze from many minds. Those nearest normalcy hastily organized a bucket brigade while others hurried after the hand-drawn pumper wagon with its pair of canvas hoses. The blast had knocked Bradley Ashton off his feet and he scrambled mindlessly in the dirt, jibbering in terror. Tanaka Tom applied round-pointed spurs to his Morgan's flanks and started in Ashton's direction.

A moment's flash of sanity returned to Bradley Ashton. He saw the looming figure, its hideous face seeming to yell at him, and he managed to regain his feet. Turning first one way, then the next, he dashed at last for his parsonage. Tom side-jumped the Morgan, cutting off Bradley Ashton's line of retreat. The sound of the blast had died, echoing away, and everyone's hearing returned to normal, registering the mournful tolling of the church bell that continued erratically as the building shuddered and settled itself into the hungry tongues of flame. A trio of deacons suddenly appeared at the opposite side of the square, rifles at the ready.

One of their bullets smashed into Tanaka Tom's armor, tearing away a *kesho notta hizu-hiki*—a sword deflecting shoulder flange. A second struck one of the horn-shaped *maedate* frontal decorations on his helmet, giving his head a painful wrench. The combined effect nearly knocked Tom from his horse. Then shots blasted from beyond the shimmering heat wave of the blazing church as Peter Miller and his companions got into the battle.

One of the gunmen died instantly, a second flung up his arms and fell wounded. Tanaka Tom swung his big Colt revolver in line with the remaining deacon and cooly shot the man. Tom's bullet entered the gunhawk's body two inches above his navel. His face took on a stupefied expression as he doubled over, toppling slowly to the ground. The momentary distraction saved Brad Ashton's life for the time being.

Ashton spun on his heel and dashed toward the only haven his confused mind could summon up. The dormitory of the Sacred Sisterhood. There he would find safety, arms, and a chance to withstand this demon. Behind him he heard the drumming of hooves and looked over his shoulder to see Tanaka Tom riding down on him once more. Clutching at any hope, Ashton bent low, taking a rifle from the hands of a dead deacon, holding it before him like a slender stave.

Tanaka Tom skidded the Morgan to a dust-boiling halt and dismounted. He advanced on a trembling Bradley Ashton, *katana* at the ready. When he closed with Ashton, he brought the sword down with whistling speed. Ashton managed an excellent parry and jumped back.

"Bradley Ashton." Tanaka Tom spoke with a voice of doom. "I want you to know why it is you must die."

"Why? W-what have I ever done . . . t-to you?"

"Remember your days with the old Two-fifty-first Ohio?" Tom struck again, Ashton deflected the blow.

"I . . . I . . . uh . . ."

"There was a small plantation on the Savannah River. Hollister and the rest of you paid it a visit. The family's name was Fletcher."

Unbidden, images filled Ashton's mind. Scenes of Spanish moss draped cypress trees, drooping, yellow-green willows. With them came remembered sounds; the screams of a young girl and her mother as an even two dozen men had their way with them. Of a tousle-headed little boy being ravaged by C. C. Steel. "So what?" he replied defensively. "What has that to do with you and me?"

"I am the only surviving member of that family; Thomas Fletcher. Everyone who harmed my family will die."

Hollister! Colonel Edward Hollister had somehow brought about this ruin of all he had dreamed of, Bradley Ashton thought in a flash. How could the evil colonel reach out over the years to smash his hopes like this? Yet this man Fletcher wouldn't be here seeking blood if Hollister hadn't led a raid against the Fletcher plantation. If it hadn't been for Hollister . . . Bradley Ashton barely managed to block Tanaka Tom's next attack. With a whimper of despair he dropped the rifle, his hands stinging from the power of Tom's attacks, and ran once again toward the porch of the Sisterhood dormitory. Tom Fletcher pounded grimly after him.

Whining in abject terror, a white line of froth bubbling on his lips, Bradley Ashton wrenched open the door and dashed inside as Tanaka Tom started up the wooden steps. The Six-gun Samurai reached the open doorway in time to hear a shriek of agony rise from Ashton. He stepped inside and saw the former lieutenant in the 251st Ohio cringing on the floor while wild-eyed little girls, ranging in age from twelve to sixteen, slashed at him with kitchen knives, wood saws and sharp, long fingernails.

Ashton screamed again as a blade bit deeply into his shoulder, tore flesh and cloth while it dragged downward to be deflected by his rib cage. In desperation Ashton pulled a derringer from a coat pocket under his robe, fumbled to draw back the hammer. Then his hand seemed to leap from his arm, thudded on the uncarpeted floor while the fingers still grasped the tiny gun. Tanaka Tom placed the slanted tip of his *katana* against the pulsating flesh of Ashton's throat and shoved violently.

Ashton's eyes bulged and he heard the hysterical screams of the vengeance-minded little girls for a few moments before Tanaka Tom twisted his blade and slashed outward. The keen edge of the Six-gun Samurai's *katana* severed the carotid artery and jugular vein on one side of Ashton's throat, spilling his life out in a red fountain.

Without a word, Tanaka Tom strode from the dormitory and mounted his horse. In the near distance Pete Miller hugged his daughters to him, a six-gun in one hand hanging at his side. At a nod from Tom Fletcher, he began calling out to the clusters of confused and still frightened people of New Caanaland.

"Ashton is dead. He was a fraud. He fooled all of us and used the poison in the peyote buds to enslave our minds. He's gone now and we're free." He gestured to Tanaka Tom, who rode silently through the gathering throng of people, out toward the road from a disintegrating New Caanaland. "It is this man who saved us. He is good, not evil. Ashton was our enemy, not him. Let him go in peace."

A lone human voice rose in faltering song, joined by others so that by the time the Six-gun Samurai reached the first low rise he could clearly hear the words they sang.

"He has loosed the fearful lightning of his terrible swift sword . . ."

Tanaka Tom Fletcher turned back toward the village, reined in. He waved to those below, a smile on his lips hidden by the mask. Things would be all right in Yellow Creek Valley, he decided. He turned to ride on and didn't pause when the belltower of Ashton's evil church gave a convulsive shudder and toppled into the raging flames, its bell clanging in discordant peals all the way to the ground.

Epilogue

"Honored Father." The graceful forms of the calligraphy flowed onto a stiff sheet of paper from the tip of the brush in Tanaka Tom Fletcher's left hand. He felt far from the composure demanded of an expert calligraphist, his mind wondering over how to phrase this letter. Alone in his room at the Palace Hotel in Denver, he felt isolated from his purpose in coming to America. He had missed Edward Hollister again, by a matter of days, and telling of his failure was difficult. He dipped the brush in the stone well of ink and began.

"So far seven men on General Tomlinson's list have died by my hand or as a result of my search for Vengeance. Yet the man most responsible continues to elude me. I am no nearer the author of my troubles than when I first set foot on American soil.

"I came here to the town they call the Mile High City following Edward Hollister. But Denver is not a small frontier village and for three days now I have sought someone who knows of Hollister or his whereabouts, but to no avail. My delay in dealing with Bradley Ashton has caused the trail to 'grow cold,' as the saying goes in this country. The depot agent for the Kansas and Pacific recalls a man of Hollister's description arriving in Denver from the west and also his departure four days ago, although he can not say in truth which direction he went.

"Hollister could have gone on to the east, a crowded area of dense population in which every man is a stranger to his neighbor. To find Hollister there would be next to impossible. In that event I must await his return to the sparsely inhabited frontier. Meanwhile I have received information from a trusted friend of General Tomlinson, a U.S. Marshal in the Utah and Nevada parts of this vast country, that Harry Kitchner, a former *socho*—sergeant major—of Hollister's 251st Ohio regiment is engaged in some sort of criminal activities in a locale little more than five hundred miles from here. It seems strange to refer to such great distances as being nearby, yet that is the case in this my homeland. Therefore, until I have a more definite lead to Hollister, I may as well make the journey to look into Kitchner's activities. For where I find him, I may also find Hollister, though I fear my quest is far from ended.

"Give my love to Joshi, my honorable mother, and to all in the noble house of Tanaka Nobunara."

A final dip of the brush and Tom Fletcher signed his letter, "Your obedient son, Tanaka Ichimara Tomi."

GLOSSARY

Bojutsu—The "Way of the Stick." A martial art based on the use of 4 and 6 foot staves.

Budo Shoshin Shu—The *Book of the Warrior's Way*, written in the 1600s by the noted samurai-philosopher, Daidoji Yuzan.

Bushido—The "Way of the Warrior." A code of conduct governing both social and military activities for the samurai class, partly written (see *Budo Shoshin Shu*), partly word-of-mouth tradition.

Butai—Detachment (military).

Butaicho—Detachment commander (captain).

Cha—Green tea in leaf form from the northern volcanic slopes of Japan.

Daimyo—Orders of nobility in Japan, with varying degrees of rank—3rd, 2nd, 1st class—corresponding to European titles—court, baron, earl.

Gehtas—Platform sandals, usually supported on two wooden blocks each.

Gohan—Hulled, white rice, boiled to a sticky consistency. The main staple of Japan.

Gomen nasi—Pardon me, excuse me.

Haiku—A Japanese poem consisting of seventeen syllables in three lines, not necessarily rhyming.

Ho-tachi—Literally, alternative sword. The short fighting sword of the samurai, with a blade of 24" length.

Iai—The art of drawing the sword.

Iaijutsu—The "Way of the Sword." The Japanese school of sword-fighting.

182

Joro—Whore. A prostitute in a common brothel.

Kami—Spirits or sprites that inhabit everything in the universe according to Shinto. The good spirits that came to man to free him from the *mikoto*.

Kamikazi—(Spirit of) the Divine Wind. A typhoon.

Karma—Fate or destiny as described by Zen and later Nichi-ren Buddhism.

Katana—Second largest sword. The *tachi*, a 5-foot blade was for ceremonial purposes and executions. The *katana*, with its 40-inch blade, is the fighting sword of the samurai.

Ki—The projected mental force behind the practice of martial arts.

Koketsu—A small, orange-fleshed, sour plum from Japan.

Konnichiwa—Good afternoon.

Kusarigama—A samurai fighting weapon consisting of a chain with a steel ball or wooden handle on one end and a sickle blade on the other.

Kusazuri—Literally: grass panties or drawers. A padded, flared skirt of overlapping fire-hardened lacquered wood strips, decorated with woven seagrass.

Kyo—The 8-foot long samurai bow.

Kyudo—The "Way of the Bow." Samurai Zen archery.

Mikoto—The Dark Spirits. Supposed to have inhabited Japan before the coming of man.

Miri-uchi—Right-strike slash. A sword cut executed from the *iai* lightning draw, in which the blade rises upward and to the right.

Musume—Girl(s).

No—And.

Obi—A cloth girdle or belt worn by men and women, often decorated and made of silk.

Rentai—Regiment (military).

Rokushakubo—Combat or fighting staff (martial arts term).

Saki—Rice wine.

Samurai—Lowest rank of peerage in old Imperial Japan. A martial title equivalent to knighthood in Europe.

Sayonara—Good-bye.

Senzuri o kakimas'—Literally: to scratch where it itches. Vulgar term for masturbation.

Seppuku—Ritual suicide for dishonor, consisting of disemboweling with the *tanto* knife by means of a crosswise stroke and upward slash of the abdomen. A friend, acting as second, would then strike the victim's head from his shoulders to insure his rebirth as a samurai.

Shogun—Highest ranking noble in old Imperial Japan. Leader of the secular government and commander of armed forces until reign of Emperor Meiji in 1868 and establishment of national army and civil parliament (the Diet).

Shohatsu—Horizontal strike with a kusarigama. Either a roundhouse or backhand delivery, giving an undulating "snap" to the sickle.

Shomen-uchi—Primary sword cut in which the weapon is held in both hands, elevated overhead, parallel to the ground on the forward step with the lead foot, brought swiftly downward on movement of the rear foot.

Sukuichi—A figure-eight movement made with the chain of a kusarigama.

Sumimasen, dozo—Excuse me, please.

Sushi—Raw fish, octopus, clams, sea slugs, and other seafood, served with rice vinegar and sugar seasoned gohan, seaweed and other condiments.

Tabi—Slippers made of cotton or silk, split-toed to accommodate a sandal thong between the big and middle toes.

Tanto—Fighting dagger of the samurai.

Tatami—Tightly braided blocks of dried seagrass used as floor covering in Japanese homes, training mats for martial arts, and as cushioning for sandals.

Tonki—Slender, leaf-bladed throwing darts, forerunners of shuriken, varying in length from four to nine inches.

Tsugi—Point following thrust. A technique in fighting with the katana in which the blade is held at an upward angle, edge parallel to the ground, allowing the opponent's momentum to drive him onto the tip.

Yokomen—A downward slanting, side-to-side cut to the base of the neck, decapitating the victim.

SIX-GUN SAMURAI

by Patrick Lee

FROM THE LAND OF THE SHOGUNS AND AMERICA'S #1 SERIES PUBLISHER, AN EXCITING NEW ACTION/ADVENTURE SERIES THAT COMBINES FAR-EASTERN TRADITION WITH HARDCORE WESTERN VIOLENCE!

Stranded in Japan, American-born Tom Fletcher becomes immersed in the ancient art of bushido—a violent code demanding bravery, honor and ultimate sacrifice—and returns to his homeland on a bloodsoaked trail of vengeance.